MONSTERS BY MISTAKE

INCLUDES THESE BOOKS:
NOW YOU SEE ME
SNAKE BELIEVE

KARLA DOYLE

CONTENTS

NOW YOU SEE ME

SNAKE BELIEVE

Now You See Me

MONSTER

Between The Sheets

KARLA DOYLE

Elise wishes she were invisible. Roan wishes he wasn't.

ROAN

At eighteen, I was a young man winning the game of life. I had a college football scholarship and a cute girl-friend on my arm for my hometown's annual Halloween party. Forget spiking the punch. The eccentric old scientist who lives in the woods brewed something more potent... and permanently life-altering.

Twenty years later, I'm not a man, I'm a monster. Invisibility isn't the superpower people think it is. It's a curse. A condition I wouldn't wish on anyone, and since the crazy old scientist doesn't know how I got this way, or if I can spread it to others, I'm not just destined to be unseen, I'm also going to be alone. That's how it has to be.

Until the night I post a grumpy "In Search Of" ad, and get a single reply. I don't know why Elise agreed to my self-serving demands of complete visual anonymity, but my life was instantly fuller because she did. I don't have to see her to fall for her. But I know it can never be more than long-distance feelings and inspiration for my right hand.

Until the day Elise surprises me by breaking our anonymity agreement and shows up in my coffee shop... and gets a monstrous surprise in return.

ELISE

People can claim otherwise, but appearances matter. I learned that after an accident left one side of my face heavily scarred. I'm used to the staring. The pointing and whispering. Kids asking their parents if I'm a monster. I'm also used to being alone, because the dating pool dried up the day I lost half my beauty.

I was searching job listings the night I found Roan's "In Search Of" post. It's been years since I read a singles ad, and I still don't know why I did. Call it coincidence, fate, or the universe doing something to balance the scales. It was as if Roan wrote that ad for me.

Every day since has been better than the one before it. My friends think Roan must be a hideous ogre to be hiding behind his "no pictures, no contact" rule. I don't care what he looks like. Roan and I click in every way–and I do mean *every*. He doesn't need to touch me in person to satisfy me. But I'd like him to.

Six months after agreeing to his conditions, I want to break them. I'm ready to take the biggest risk of my life–rejection by the man I love. I want all of Roan Byrne. The good, the sexy, and if he does turn out to be an ogre, the ugly. I only hope that when he sees me, he feels the same way...

Chapter One

ROAN

Crisp autumn air greets me as I exit Lucky Beans just before nine o'clock. The night sky hangs over Screaming Woods like a dark blanket. Clouds block any starlight, and the sliver of a moon offers the barest hint of luminescence.

Twenty years ago, I wouldn't have noticed the state of the sky. I was focused on a future that included big-city bright lights, not the endless sky above Screaming Woods, the only place I'll ever be able to call home. Monsters didn't exist back then. Not in this town, anyway. Now, monsters *are* the town. And I'm one of them.

People say I got lucky. Those of us who drank the

punch at our town's annual Halloween celebration that fateful night all morphed into different things. Wolf man, ogre, naga, orc, gargoyle, zombie, hell boy, minotaur, dragon, electric man... the list goes on. I didn't grow a tail, scales, fur, or fangs. I didn't develop superhuman powers. I disappeared.

One minute, I was an eighteen-year-old with a football scholarship and a cute girlfriend tucked under my arm. Then that arm, along with the rest of me, vanished from view. All hell broke loose when the transformations happened. Nobody goes to a Halloween party thinking they'll leave as a real-life monster. For those of us who sampled Dr. Karloff's homebrew, that's exactly what happened.

Most of the normal human residents fled town. Some immediately following the event, some later, when it became clear the crazy old scientist in the woods couldn't figure out how to undo the damage he'd caused. Those of us who changed that night had no choice but to stay. The world beyond our town's boundaries isn't ready for what we've become. And those of us who are monsters aren't interested in being lab rats.

I don't know where life would've taken me if I hadn't become invisible. Maybe I would've ended up taking over my family's coffee shop, regardless. But I would've made use of that football scholarship and gone to college first. I would've had options.

I'm damn sure I wouldn't have ended up a solitary man with only my hand for company at the end of the day. Twenty years after drinking Dr. Karloff's concoction, that's exactly how it is, though.

That's how it has to be. Touching, kissing, fucking... I can't do any of those things. The crazy scientist doesn't know why soft, porous objects turn invisible when I touch them. Doesn't have the slightest damn clue about any of the changes he caused. Says he thought he created a "good mood" elixir that'd be the hit of the party. Not by a longshot, doc.

One thing I do know—I won't risk infecting another person with this condition. I'm not that much of a monster.

My house is a short walk from my business, and I'm about halfway when a couple steps out of one of the downtown pubs. They can't see me, so I step off the sidewalk as we cross paths.

They're both bird people—fully bird from the waist up, human legs on the bottom—and they're talking in a unique combination of chirping and words. One looks like a yellow finch, the other looks like a hawk. I have no idea if they kept their human anatomy below the belt. Those kinds of details don't make the gossip rounds in the coffee shop. We're a pretty tightknit community now that most of the residents are monsters.

Regardless of their bird-to-human body ratio, the hawk and finch people are alike. Able to understand what the other one is going through. Sharing the same existence. I'm happy they have each other in this fucked-up reality we're all living. That doesn't stop envy from twisting in my gut when the hawk extends one wing around the back of the finch.

I miss physical contact. Sex—fuck yes, I miss that. I'd only had an introduction before becoming a monster. But innocent contact, too. Holding hands. Hugging. Simple touches. It is what it is. And it's not going to change since I'm the only person in town who pulled a vanishing act on monster-making night.

My phone chimes in my pocket as I turn onto my street. I know without looking that it's Elise, yet my pulse picks up when I see her name on the lock screen. We message daily. For hours, every night after I close the coffee shop, and our conversations are the highlight of every day.

I've spent a lot of time in chat rooms over the years, and always logged out feeling lonelier than when I logged on. I knocked back a bit too much of the Jameson after one of those logouts, and posted a wide-ranging "In Search Of" ad I'm not proud of.

ISO single, non-superficial woman with intelligence and a sense of humor. Bonus points for a dirty mind, if only for the sake of fun conversation. Cybersex optional, but not required. Online, visually anonymous communication only. No in-person meet ups, no video chats, no exchange of pictures. My appearance is off-limits, and in return, yours is completely unimportant to me. Terms are non-negotiable.
—Unlucky Giant Leprechaun

I didn't include any sort of bio. Just my grumpy list of demands and a stupid sign off. Asshole much? The next day's sober me cringed at the sight of it. By then, the ad had several hundred views. Unsurprisingly, my inbox wasn't overflowing with offers to get acquainted. But there was one response.

Dear Unlucky Giant Leprechaun,
I meet your criteria and I accept your terms. Let's arrange a time to chat. Maybe we'll both be luckier for it.
—Pot of Tarnished Gold

If she'd signed it Elise, I probably would've deleted the message without another thought. It was "Pot of Tarnished Gold" that got me. I knew right then we were going to hit it off. And we did.

Six months later, we're still hitting it off. Sometimes we discuss big stuff. Others, we talk for hours about nothing. There's flirting and affection, and on a few occasions, it's gotten explicit enough that I've had to tap my messages with one hand. Our relationship is a mix of comfortable friendship, intellectual connection, and chemistry. Hard to believe all of that's possible with strictly online communication, but it is.

It's even better now that we've switched to regular texting instead of meeting in a chat room. The rules are still in place, but we're in touch constantly. Little messages throughout the day. Normal relationship stuff—aside from the never-seeing-each-other part.

That's always going to suck. But this is as real as it gets for me.

I open her text as soon as I'm in my house. Between the darkness and my invisibility, nobody can see the grin on my face, but I like privacy just the same. No one in my day-to-day life knows about Elise and I plan to keep it that way. People have accepted that the invisible man is a loner. I don't need anyone encouraging me to try having more.

> **ELISE:**
> Hi! 😊 Let me know when you're home. I have something personal to talk to you about, and I don't want to distract you while you're at work.

Any message from Elise gets my blood pumping. This one diverts it straight to my cock.

> **ME:**
> Just walked in. You have my full attention.

Emphasis on full, because my dick is at standing at attention when I strip out of my clothes. Phone in one hand, hard dick in the other, I settle on the bed. Bring on the personal, not-suitable-for-work stuff. I'm more than ready.

Dots march in the bubble on Elise's side of the screen. Then stop. Then begin again. And repeat, repeat, repeat.

I fight the urge to send her another message. You'd

think patience would be one of my better virtues by now, but since Elise came into my life, I've reverted to having the patience of a lovesick, horny eighteen-year-old.

Finally, her text pops onto the screen. But it's not the lengthy bubble I expected after all those dots. Or the kind of message I had in mind.

> **ELISE:**
> I'd like to talk to you. Really talk. How do you feel about us having phone calls? Just voice, no video calls.

Actual calls with Elise. I'd be lying if I said I haven't wondered what she sounds like. I've also wondered what she looks like. There have been times I've been tempted to ask for a picture, but that'd be breaking the rules I set out. It'd also open the door for her to want a picture in return. Something I literally can't give, ever.

But that's not what she asked for.

There's no harm in taking things to the level she wants. I know from our hundreds of text and email conversations that she has a great sense of humor. I'd love to hear her laugh. To be the person who makes her laugh out loud.

Plus, phone sex. The things we could do. Goddamn, I'd love to hear what she sounds like when she comes.

> **ME:**
> Let's do it. I'd love to hear your voice.

I hit Send before the reality of what I'm agreeing to overtakes my longing for the *more* I can never truly have.

ELISE:
How about now? Before I lose my nerve?

My booming laugh echoes in the silence of my empty house.

ME:
Yeah, now is great. And I know what you mean.

ELISE:
You're nervous too?

ME:
Hell yeah. Talking to you is the highlight of my day. I don't want to screw up and scare you off.

ELISE:
Nothing about you could scare me off.

I grunt and look at the phone, which appears to be floating in the air, rather than sitting in the palm of my hand. Everything about me would terrify her. But she'll never know that.

I'm an intelligent enough guy. Pretty personable, too. Years of running a busy coffee shop have given me plenty of practice making spontaneous conversation. Yet, when the phone rings in my hand and Elise's name lights the screen, I suddenly have no idea what to say. It's been a damn long time since I talked to a woman who matters. And Elise matters.

By the second ring, my pulse is pounding against my temples, and my hands are clammy. I'm a thirty-eight-year-old man and I don't know how to answer a phone call. Fuck me.

"Hello," I say, shaking my head at the total lack of originality or finesse.

"Hi." One little word in her soft, feminine voice is all it takes to send sparks racing through me. Then she laughs, and the brief sound ignites those sparks, setting me on fire. "You wouldn't believe how nervous I am. I feel like a teenager calling the guy she's crushing on."

"Glad I'm not the only one," I say, chuckling. "And if you're crushing on me, I'm the luckiest guy around, at any age."

"Ooh... you're as charming on the phone as you are in messages."

So far, so good. Makes me wish we'd done this

sooner. "I've wondered about your voice lots of times. It's very pretty."

"Thank you. Yours is..." Too many seconds of silence beat by.

"Don't leave me hanging here. You can say goodbye and end the call. We can go back to messaging." *And it'll never be the same.*

"No, I want to keep talking to you. It's silly, really, but your voice took me by surprise. You told me your parents are from Ireland, but since you were born here, I didn't expect you to have any accent."

"It's light compared to theirs. But I learned to speak while listening to them, so some of it snuck in."

"Well, I like it. Your voice is like dessert for my ears. And now I'm even more jealous of the customers in your coffee shop, because they get to hear your voice all the time."

"No need to be jealous of anyone. No one in town takes notice of my voice or anything else about me. Even if they did, I'm not interested."

"It's selfish that I like hearing that, but I do." Another laugh floats into my ear. "Listen to me, possessively staking my claim on you. It's so unlike me. I don't even recognize myself."

Now it's my turn to laugh, only mine is more of a grunt. I wonder if I'd recognize myself if I woke up to a reflection in the mirror.

"Do you have red hair?" A strangled gasp follows her question. "I'm sorry, that slipped out. I know appearances are off-limits. I've always wondered because of the leprechaun comment in your original ad, then finding out your family is Irish, but I blame hearing you have an accent for the slipup. You don't have to answer."

If I'm careful, what could it hurt? "I was a solid ginger all the way through high school. Less so now."

"I'm sure you're still handsome, regardless of your current hair color."

"I couldn't say."

"I wouldn't expect you to," she says. "You're not a cocky or self-centered man. That's been clear since our first conversation."

I cover the phone with my palm to mask my grunt. She has no idea how *clear* I am.

"I have long, light-brown hair with some subtle, soft-pink highlights. I know you don't care, and maybe you didn't want to know, but—"

"I want to know everything, Elise. There are a lot of things I won't ask because I agreed not to when we started out and I'm a man of my word. But anything you choose to share with me, I'm here for it."

"Anything? Are you sure?"

"Absolutely anything. Big or small, intimately personal or casually trivial. Nothing you could tell me will change the way I feel." Except to make me fall for her even more. But it's too soon to tell her that. Hell, the time may never be right.

"Okay, here goes." She takes a deep breath, then releases it slowly. "I haven't been in a relationship or had any kind of date for nearly ten years."

My eyebrows rise and my cock throbs in my fist. I like that information more than I probably should. "It's been twenty for me." The admission I never expected to make slides from my tongue as if I'm stating my favorite color. I'm *that* comfortable with her.

"Are you serious or mocking me?"

"Serious. I'd never mock you." Fuck it, I've gone this far. Might as well open the door a little wider. "There was a chemical incident in town and I was affected."

"It changed your appearance?" she asks softly.

"Drastically."

"Mine was a car accident. The scars are... significant. People either stare or avoid looking at me altogether. Little kids point and ask their parents if I'm a monster."

Fury like I haven't felt in years flares to life, launching me to my feet. The past is beyond my control, but I could change the future. I'm the invisible man. I could follow Elise and she'd never know I was there. But the assholes who treat her badly would damn sure know. I could do whatever I want and get away with it.

"Where do you live?" The question is out of my mouth before common sense kicks in. "Shit. Sorry. That was way out of bounds. Forget I asked."

"What would you do with the information if I told you?"

"My initial impulse was to quietly stalk you and punish the people who disrespect you."

Her laugh fills my ear, loosening the knot inside me. "You think I wouldn't notice a ginger-haired giant leprechaun tailing me?"

"My stealth mode is pretty effective."

"If you say so," she says, laughing until she sighs. "I appreciate your desire to protect me, but I don't need it. And... if ever you *were* to come find me, I'd want it to be for positive reasons. I wouldn't want you to hide. I'd want to see you."

Just like that, the knot is back. "I'd want that too."

"Maybe one day?" Her voice is so gentle, so hopeful.

"You never know," I say. But I do know. I just care about her too much to tell her it'll never happen.

Chapter Two

ELISE

As a transcriptionist, focus and accuracy are key. I usually excel in both areas. Not today. I've restarted my current project multiple times and have yet to reach the halfway point of the audio. My mind keeps wandering to Roan.

We spent nearly two hours on the phone last night. There were a few moments near the beginning where it got a bit intense. Roan has always been so easygoing in our chats; I didn't expect him to get growly and protective. But I liked it. A lot. I haven't had a man care about me in that way since before the accident.

After that, we settled into nonstop conversation.

About his coffee shop. My job. Lots of things we had already discussed in our previous chat messages, yet hearing it all in his rich voice made it feel brand new.

Though I'd never wish harm or trauma on anyone, discovering we're both physically scarred gave me hope I never expected to feel. Knowing Roan and I share the same reason for hiding our appearances has fueled my courage to cross another line. Since I'm clearly not getting through this audio document anytime soon, I might as well take that step now.

I save my work, set my equipment aside, then scroll through the photos saved on my phone. I attach the most recent pre-accident picture I have, taken the day of my accident, at a friend's wedding. It's a candid, full-face shot with a beaming smile. I look happy because I was happy. My life was full and I had grand plans to enjoy every minute.

If only I'd taken the next cab that night. Or the one before. I spent a lot of angry, lonely years wondering why fate put me in *that* taxi—the one destined for a head-on collision less than three blocks from the banquet hall. What had I done to deserve such an ugly —literally ugly—twist of fate?

Now I know the reason fate plucked me off course. Without the accident and everything that followed, I wouldn't have met Roan. Despite what my friends think, I know he's the one. And... I think he knows it, too.

My finger hovers over the Send button. I've composed a "hey, no pressure" message in my head to send along with the picture. As true as the sentiment might be, if I send this photo, he's going to feel pressured. To tell me I'm attractive. To reciprocate with a picture that I know he doesn't want to send. I could ruin everything.

"Shit." I remove the image from the message, shut off the phone, then slump over my desk. I thought having an online relationship would be enough. Then I thought talking on the phone would be enough. Wrong on both counts. The more of Roan I get, the more I want.

My phone chimes from its abandoned position to the left of my bowed head. I'm upright in a heartbeat because it's Roan's tone. He's usually too busy with work to message mid-day. My pulse is hammering by the time I unlock the phone and get to our message thread. According to my friends, it's crazy to be this wrapped up in a relationship with a faceless man. I know they think I'm just lonely and desperate, willing to accept whatever attention I can get. But they don't know Roan.

> **ROAN:**
> I haven't stopped thinking about you
> since you said goodbye last night.

I clutch my chest and squeal like a lovestruck girl. Totally accurate.

ME:
Same. I have eight hours of legal droning to transcribe and I can't focus on a single word. It's your fault because I just want to hear your voice in my ear.

One perk of an online-only relationship—it's easier to be bold.

ROAN:
Then call me.

ME:
Now? Aren't you working at the coffee shop?

ROAN:
Yes, now. I got sent home because distracted me kept messing up the orders.

I laugh out loud while rising from my desk chair.

ME:
How can you get sent home when you own the business?

ROAN:
My full-time employee is a force to be reckoned with. She told me to go, so I went.

It's not the first time he's mentioned his female

employee. As it has before, jealousy sours my stomach and clouds my head with doubts.

> **ROAN:**
> Why isn't my phone ringing yet?

The knot in my chest loosens, and I tap the Call button.

He answers on the first ring. "Finally."

"You say that as if I kept you waiting for eternity," I say, laughing as I get comfortable on my bed.

"It feels that way."

Just like that, the doubts and jealousy dissolve. "For me, too."

"I never would've asked to shift our relationship beyond the original boundaries, but I'm damn glad you did."

Fresh courage and hope bloom in my chest. Saving those for later, when I revisit those boundaries again. "Since we're playing hooky because of our mutual distraction, we should probably make the most of this unexpected free time."

There's a beat of silence before he asks, "What did you have in mind?" Huskiness laces his voice, and the sound of rustling fabric in the background is unmistakable.

"How about twenty questions, but if you don't want to answer, you have to take a dirty dare?"

His deep chuckle sends a ripple of awareness straight between my legs. "I'm ready, but you might not be once you hear my questions—and my dares."

"Oh, I think I can handle anything you've got." I smile as his chuckle fills my ear, then put the phone on speaker and prop it on the pillow beside me. "I put you on speaker. Can you hear me?"

"As if you're right here in the room with me."

"I'd like that very much," I say softly.

"You have no idea how much I wish that were possible."

That's what I needed to hear. Soon, I'll make that wish a reality. Right now, we have a game to play. "Who goes first?"

A masculine sound that's part growl, part grunt sifts through the line. "Ladies always go first. No matter the place or circumstances."

"Chivalry is alive and well in... where do you live?"

"Is that your first question?"

"It is," I say, managing to keep the wobble out of my voice. "And I'm fully aware it's overstepping our boundaries of anonymity. If you don't want to answer, you're welcome to choose a dare instead."

"Screaming Woods."

I narrow my eyes at the phone. "Is that some pre-Halloween joke?"

"No joke. There's nothing funny about Screaming Woods. Well, aside from open-mic night at Down the Rabbit Hole."

"Is that a comedy club?"

"If you really want to know, you'll can ask at your next question. It's my turn now."

"Ask away," I say, rolling onto my side.

"When was your last orgasm?"

Heat floods my face and I sputter as if I'm choking on my tongue. Lying isn't my style, but I'm not telling him about the scratch-that-itch break I took less than an hour ago. I swallow purposefully, then squeak out a response. "Dare, please."

His deep chuckle rumbles through the speaker. "That's an answer in itself. But you're not off the hook. I dare you to get naked."

"Maybe I'm already naked."

"And maybe I'll dare you to send me visual proof when you don't answer my next question."

My jaw literally drops. We've shared some smoking-hot text sessions, but hearing him say sexy things takes it to another level. And for him to even hint at getting a nude... Maybe *he's* testing the flexibility of our boundaries, too.

I wiggle out of my yoga pants, sweatshirt, and underwear. I arrange the pink bikini panties to look seductive, then pick up my phone and snap a picture.

"You won't have to make that dare," I say, then hit Send.

ME:
<pic of clothes>

A gruff sound rumbles through the speaker. "You're naked right now?"

"That was your dare. But I kept my socks on. It's October. If my feet get cold, that's all I can think about, and I'd rather be thinking of other things right now."

"Definitely keep the socks on," he says, chuckling. "Your turn."

"I think it's only fair to ask you the same question."

"Then ask it," he says.

"I just did."

"I didn't hear a question. And I want to. I want to hear the sexy words in your soft voice. Ask the question, Elise."

A shiver ripples through me, and it has nothing to do with being cold. It's not his turn, yet he's essentially daring me to talk dirty to him.

Unspoken dare accepted. "When was the last time you stroked your cock until you came?"

His groan fills my bedroom. "Jesus, that's hot."

Feminine confidence I haven't felt in a decade blooms inside me. "And *that* wasn't an answer."

His perfectly masculine chuckle sends sparks skittering through my body. "It was this morning."

"Taking care of the morning wood?" I ask, even though my turn is over.

"The morning wood from dreaming about you. Then again in the shower, because I was still hard from thinking about you."

"I know I've been celibate a long time, but I've never been with a guy who can get the job done twice before breakfast."

"You were with the wrong guys."

And now I'm with the right one.

"We're done playing the question game," he says in a low, rough tone.

"We are?"

"Yes. I have a thousand questions I could and will ask, but not right now. I've been imagining how you feel and the way you taste for close to half a year. So we're going to play the happy ending game."

"Is that what I think it is?" My voice sounds like a phone-sex operator. No surprise, since I'm a puddle of turned-on neediness.

"If you think it's you touching yourself until you come, then yes. And I'm going to enjoy every sexy word, breath, and sound you make."

Holy hell. Unless I fake a bad connection and hang up, this is happening. "I want you to have a happy ending, too."

"You want to hear me grunting and groaning your name while I fuck my fist?"

"God, yes." I slide my hand between my legs, biting my bottom lip when the need to come flares beneath my touch. "If you're not naked already, get naked."

Rustling fabric and a distinctive metallic zip accompanies his throaty chuckle. "Done. My turn to tell you what to do, sweetheart. Hand between your legs, where my tongue and cock should be. Tell me what you're doing. Every detail."

"I'm rubbing my clit with two fingers," I say, tipping my hips up as the orgasm begins to build. "Hard and fast—God, I can feel it starting."

"Not yet, baby. Not yet." The sound of slick slapping and masculine breathing drifts through the speaker, filling my head as if he were here with me.

"Lick your fingers. Tell me how wet you are, what your pussy tastes like."

My body cries at its loss as I stop just shy of crashing over the edge. I lick up and down my fingers, humming as I suck them into my mouth. "Tangy, so wet for your cock," I say, licking my lips as I slip my hand between my legs again. I'm more sensitive now, and moan aloud the instant I touch my clit. "I need to come," I pant, rubbing faster, harder. "Roan, I can't wait... have to... *oh God, yes*..."

His deep moan joins mine, then tapers off to a husky chuckle. "Fuck, woman. Holy shit—so hot."

Heat flushes through me as I pull the blankets over me. "You, too. We should do that again."

"Not should, will."

"When?" It's silly to feel needy, but I do.

"How about every day, for the rest of time? Too much to ask?"

"Sounds perfect to me," I whisper.

"Me too, sweetheart. Me too."

CHAPTER THREE

ELISE

"Are you absolutely sure about this?" my best friend asks as we walk to my car. "Showing up on the doorstep of a guy you've never met, or even seen, is kind of out there."

"You make me sound like a stalker."

"It's him I'm worried about, not you. You don't know anything about this guy. Not really. He could be stringing you along, only telling you what you want to hear. He might be a total loser in real life. And he's too secretive, Ellie Belle. Not showing you a single picture? Those are glaring red flags. What if he's some kind of hideous monster? Or worse. He could be a serial killer, for all you know."

"He's a coffee shop owner who's guarded about his looks because a chemical accident disfigured him. If anyone understands how he feels, it's me. We have tons in common, get along great, and there's a boat-load of chemistry. I don't care what he looks like. If I get there and *my* face is an issue for him..." I shrug because I don't have a plan for that scenario.

"Then you'll say 'good riddance' to his dumb ass and forget about him," Anne says, pulling me into a hug.

"Right." I swallow the lump in my throat. Even my bestie, who loves me unconditionally, won't reassure me about my appearance. Just this once, I wouldn't mind if she lied.

ELISE

My car is only a few years old, yet the built-in navigation system refused to recognize any of the addresses in Screaming Woods that I got from the internet. Addresses that didn't show up in my first Google search—or any of the half dozen that followed. No matter how many variations of wording I entered, I came up empty. No results for the town of Screaming Woods or its coffee shop called Lucky Beans.

It was as if the town didn't want to be found. Then,

one night, after another amazing conversation with Roan lasted for hours and left me smiling so much, my face literally ached—I opened my laptop and searched one more time. And voilà... results. The town's location. A street address and phone number for Lucky Beans. And more.

Fortunately, I printed all the information while I had the chance. Good old-fashioned map to the rescue. Many hours of twists and turns later, I'm in Screaming Woods. Somewhere among the streets unfolding ahead, so is Roan.

Just knowing we're in the same place sends my heart racing. I've been thinking about this moment nearly since the beginning of my online relationship with Roan. He believes he's unlovable in person because of what he described as a drastic change to his appearance. Drastic is a vague and intense word, so I've imagined a lot of possibilities. None of them scare me. I know his exterior won't change what's in my heart. Only our face-to-face meeting will prove that to him. And hopefully, he'll feel the same way.

It's nearly five o'clock, meaning Lucky Beans is open and Roan is likely there. I recognize the street names from the street map I've spent the last few nights studying, and I'm probably five minutes from the coffee shop. At the next intersection, I fight temptation and turn in a different direction, toward the motel where I've reserved a room. Must stick to the plan.

I park in front of the motel, and hold my head

high as I walk toward the door beneath the Open sign. Screaming Woods is considerably smaller than the city I left behind. It's possible the residents here have never seen a face as badly scarred as mine. I pause at the entrance and draw a deep breath. Whatever happens on the other side of this door, I'm ready.

"Hello there! Welcome to The Sunnyside Motel."

I freeze in my tracks, my bottom lip dropping at the sight of the—*man?*—behind the desk. Yes, he's a man. He has arms, a torso, and legs, from what I can see. But his face is smooth and flat, his eyes sit more to the sides than the front, and his lipless mouth stretches around the sides of his earless, scaly head. Tomorrow is Halloween, but his appearance doesn't look like a costume. It's too real. The man waiting for me to answer is a snake. Literally.

"You must be Elise Hawthorne," he says, drawing the "s" out in a subtle hiss.

"Yes, that's me." I shake my head to free up my stuck eyeballs. Shame on me for staring. "How do you know who I am?"

"Out-of-town reservations are quite rare here."

"At The Sunnyside Motel?" I ask, moving closer.

He shakes his head as I reach the desk. "In Screaming Woods. People who come here tend to have a specific reason for the visit."

"I have a specific reason." The best reason—love. "I met someone online, and he lives here. He doesn't know I'm coming, though. So please don't tell anyone you have a guest from out of town. I'd hate for it to get back to him and ruin the surprise."

"You have my utmost discretion, Ms. Hawthorne."

"Thank you. And please call me Elise. Also, I apologize for staring when I walked in. My friend, the man I'm here to surprise, told me there was a chemical incident in town years ago, but I didn't realize its effects were widespread."

"A chemical incident." The man tilts his head, studying me with his unblinking eyes. "That's as good a description as any, I suppose. And it explains your easy acceptance of my condition. What monster did your friend become?"

My spine stiffens, a reflex response to the word *monster*, despite his casual and nonjudgmental use. Plus, to call Roan a monster when this man himself is part snake...

"I don't know what he looks like," I say. "We haven't exchanged pictures."

"But you knew he had changed, and sought him out, sight unseen." The tip of his black, forked tongue slips out, then what must be the snake equivalent of a smile shifts the line of his mouth. "That takes a special person. Now I understand how you found us." He retrieves a key from a cabinet behind the desk, then dangles it in front of me. "Room five is ready for you. If you have questions or concerns about anything, don't be afraid to call the desk. I'm happy to be at your service, anytime."

"Thank you," I say, focusing on his face, rather

than the coolness of his snakeskin-covered hand when our fingers graze. "Would you like me to pay for the room now, or give you my credit card for a deposit, at least, since I'm not sure how many nights I'll be staying?"

He shakes his head, a hissing laugh rising from an open mouth that reveals his snake-fang teeth. "We'll sort that out later. Welcome to the neighborhood, Elise."

ROAN

Even in the off-peak hours, Lucky Beans is rarely empty. The coffee shop has been a town staple since my parents opened it, and that didn't change when a chunk of the local population became monsters. Survival is engrained in the Byrne family. My parents didn't morph into monsters twenty years ago, but they pivoted regardless. A week after the Halloween festival that changed everything, Lucky Beans had a new menu board with beverages to suit every newly acquired taste in town—and I do mean *every*.

Brewed drinks made from ground birdseed instead of coffee beans or tea leaves. Espresso with a shot of ethically obtained blood. Slushy drinks made from frozen, puréed slugs and earthworms. And so on.

A big chunk of the human population abandoned town after the mass transformation. Not my parents. They stayed to support me while I found my footing in a life where I'd never see my feet again. Then continued catering to every customer without bias. Just the same neighborly, honest service they'd always provided.

That's how I operate Lucky Beans, too. Taking care of my clientele is why I'm in the stockroom unboxing a shipment that literally just arrived. Either my zombie customer up front has incredibly coincidental timing, or he could sniff out the delivery of locally sourced, fresh cow brains as the truck drove through town.

I'm on my way to the front of the shop with a shrink-wrapped package of spongy pink brain meat when I hear the voice I'd recognize anywhere. The voice that's been in my ear every night since our first phone call. The voice that makes my pulse kick up a couple notches, and diverts all available blood to my cock.

"Hi... I'm looking for Roan," Elise says to Melinda, my full-time employee. "Can I see him?"

"Can you see him?" Melinda is an amazing employee. She's also an overprotective friend. "Are you kidding?"

"No, or I wouldn't have asked." Elise's voice is surprisingly calm and steady considering she's face to face with an agitated monster.

From my hiding place on the opposite side of the doorway, I hear Mel's teeth chatter. Not a good sign.

When Melinda unknowingly drank the monster-making punch, short quills sprouted from her skin. When she's calm, they lay relatively flat, like short fur. But when her emotions are heightened, those quills bristle up like a battle-ready porcupine. The chattering sound is part of the physical response.

I don't know why Elise is in my shop, but I can't go out there. Retreating deeper into the stockroom, I carefully close the office door, pull my phone from my pocket and call Lucky Beans' number. The line rings out front—once, twice, three times. Shit.

Finally, Mel answers. Since we have caller I.D., she knows it's me. "Lucky Beans," she says in a tight tone. "How can I help you?"

"Hey. Sorry to abandon you out there. I'm in the office. The woman who's looking for me is a friend. Actually—" I blow out a breath. "She's a lot more than a friend. But it's been online, and completely non-visual. She doesn't know I'm invisible, or about monsters."

"Hmm... Yes, that used to be the case, but the latter portion of the menu has changed," Mel says. "You should come and check it out in person. I think you'd be surprised at the options available to you now."

I grunt at the coded message. "Not happening. Tell her I'm not here. That you're not sure when I'll be back, or if it will be today. Get rid of her, but be nice about it, please. She's a good person, and she's important."

Mel makes a purely human, clearly disapproving

tongue-clicking sound. "Well, I hope you change your mind and come by before we sell out of something *important* you'd clearly love."

I cringe as dead air replaces Mel's disappointed voice. I silence my phone and leave it on the desk, then remove the metal-mesh barista apron and gloves I wear. Going out the rear door would be safer, but I walk into the front of the shop instead. I never would've asked Elise for a picture. Now that she's here, I can't resist seeing her. And the moment I do, I feel as if I've been sucker punched.

She's beautiful. So damn beautiful.

"I wish I could tell you," Mel says to her. "Roan had to chicken out. Wait, that's not the saying. *Duck out.* He had to duck out. I'm not even sure if he'll be back."

"He was here a few minutes ago," my oh so helpful zombie customer offers. "He went in the back to unpack a shipment of brains that just came in. And I know they were delivered. I can smell them."

Elise's gaze widens as she turns to look at the gray-skinned man.

"Cow brains," Atticus says. "Roan and Mel whip them with cinnamon to make a topping for my drinks. It's delicious. High in protein and ketogenic-diet friendly, too. Totally safe for human consumption."

"I'll keep that in mind." She gives Atticus a friendly smile before turning back to Melinda. "I apologize for disturbing your workday. Can you keep my visit a secret? Roan's not expecting me, and I really want to surprise him with a face-to-face meeting."

"That's going to be one heck of a surprise." Mel flashes her rodent-like incisors in an unusual yet unmistakable smile.

The color drains from the smooth areas of Elise's face, and every part of her expression turns down. She hurries toward the front door without another word.

"I'll be back," I whisper to Mel as I pass. Tailing Elise borders on creepy, but I am a monster, after all. I need to know where she's going. More than that, I need to know she's okay.

She walks at a brisk clip, glancing around before ducking into the nearest alley. Alone in the semi-dark, she presses her back to the brick wall and sobs. "I shouldn't have come here. *Of course* he'll be surprised by my face. Surprised and repulsed."

Fuck. I have two options here—be a monster or be a man. And I can't be a man without revealing my monstrous truth—and potentially losing her forever.

"Don't cry," I say, because manning up is the only choice.

Her body stiffens as she scans what appears to be an empty alley. "Roan?"

"I'm here."

"Where? I don't see anyone, or... any creatures." She pushes off the wall, narrowing her gaze and inspecting every inch of the visible space. "Are you a chameleon? Am I looking right at you?" She gasps before I can answer, hiding behind her hands. "It's too late, isn't it? You've already seen my face."

Instinct screams within me. To get rid of the

distance between us, pull her hands from her face, and kiss her until it's impossible for her to think anything other than the truth. I can't do any of those things. I can only tell her. "Your face is beautiful."

"You don't have to lie, Roan. I'm not foolish enough to believe it anyway. I see myself in the mirror every day."

"I don't." There's no way to avoid the truth now. Might as well get it out and over with. "I haven't had a reflection for twenty years."

She spreads her fingers enough that I can see her wide eyes. "Are you a vampire? I'm assuming vampires are real, based on everything I've seen since I arrived in town."

"There are vampires here, but I'm not one. I wish I were."

"Why would you wish that?"

"If I were a vampire, or anything other than what I am, you'd be able to see me. And I'd be able to touch you. Hold you. Kiss you."

She lowers her hands, giving me a view of her entire face and the sorrowful expression playing across it. "Are you a ghost?"

"No," I say with a grunt. "I'm still alive, just invisible."

She pushes away from the wall, moving closer, despite being unable to see me. "Then why can't you touch me?"

"Why would you want me to? I'm a freak who can never give you a normal relationship or fulfilling life."

"You're wrong. I've been happier in the last six months than I have been in years." She steps closer, her gaze searching for some hint of me that I know she'll never find. "Were all those conversations and intimate moments we shared real or an illusion?"

One lie is all it'll take to break her heart and send her back to her life. It's the best thing I could do for her. "They were real. All of them."

She's close enough for me to smell her light floral scent. Like a fool, I inhale deeply. Audibly.

Her pretty eyes open wide, and she reaches for the source of the sound—my face.

Either I'm too slow, or too selfish, because her fingers graze my cheek. A fleeting touch I shouldn't have allowed to happen.

"I can't be with you," I say, moving away. "I'm a monster, Elise. Go home. Forget me and this place. Live a normal life."

A bitter laugh rises from her lips. "I told you what my *normal* life was like. The staring, the comments, the loneliness. *I* was the monster. I've been in this town less than twenty-four hours and I feel more at home than I have in a decade. At the motel, the grocery story, walking down the street—nobody cares about my face. I'm normal here. I understand if you don't want to be with me now that you've seen me. Lucky Beans is your place and I won't go back there, but I've decided to move to Screaming Woods."

I'm still processing her words as she turns and heads out of the alley. She knows what I am and doesn't care. This should be the happiest moment of my life, only it can't be. Even though she's here to stay, I can't be with her. Not the way she deserves.

"Elise," I call, my voice booming in the silence of the alley.

She stops and turns, seeing through me as she looks right at me.

"I meant what I said. I see the scars on your skin, but they don't change the fact that you're the most beautiful woman in the world. I'm the reason we can't be together. But I'm glad you're here, and that you feel like you've found a place you belong."

She waits a few seconds, sighing when she realizes I'm finished talking. "Is that all you want to say?"

Not by a longshot. But I'm not selfish enough to say the rest of what's in my heart. "Come by Lucky Beans anytime. All the time. Your order will always be on the house. I'll make sure Melinda knows, too."

"I'll keep it in mind," she says, then turns and walks out of the alley.

I let her go because it's the best thing I can do for her. Unfortunately, it feels like the worst thing for me.

Chapter Four

ROAN

"Are you really going to keep doing this?" Melinda asks, snapping a towel in front of my face—and quite accurately, considering she can't see my face.

"Doing what?"

"Pining after your woman. Pointlessly pining after, since she couldn't make it any more obvious that she wants you to go over there and claim her."

"She's an independent woman, Mel. She doesn't want to be claimed."

My longtime employee and friend snorts under her breath. "Either you're as blind as you are invisible, or you're completely clueless, because that beautiful, intelligent, sweet, independent woman over there definitely wants you to claim her—heart, soul, and body."

My cock likes the idea. A lot. Too much, since I have a couple more hours of work before I can go home and jerk off while thinking about the woman I'll never be able to claim, even if she wanted me to.

"She can probably feel you staring at her, you know."

I jerk to face Mel. "What makes you think I was looking at her?"

"Because you're in love with her. You can't look anywhere else. Hell, *I* can feel you staring, and I'm not the object of your affection." Mel's dark eyes bore into me, as if she can actually see me.

There's no point in denying it. "It doesn't matter how I feel. You know why I can't be with her."

"But she doesn't, because you didn't do her the service of telling her everything. She put herself out there, literally in every way, by coming to Screaming Woods. I think she deserves to know the whole story. Maybe you can make things work somehow—like date but not touch, then go to your individual homes and have phone sex, or something like that. And if not, at least find your way to being friends, since she's moving here. What have you got to lose at this point?"

I've never been great at taking advice. "You're right." I grit my teeth when Mel gives me a victorious grin. "Is it possible for you to not gloat about it?"

"Are you kidding? I cherish these moments." She

snaps her towel at me again. "Stop procrastinating and get your invisible ass over there."

"Fine. No eavesdropping," I say, pointing at her, my gloved hand visible to anyone who might be looking our way.

"No guarantees on that!" Mel's voice rises to a volume that attracts attention from the handful of customers sitting at tables, including Elise. Which is probably exactly what Mel hoped to achieve.

Elise's gaze is focused on me—or more accurately, on my apron and gloves—as I walk toward her. When I reach her table, she tips her head upward, smiling as she levels her attention above the top of my apron. "Thank you for the pumpkin-spice latte. I tried to pay for it, but Melinda refused to take my money."

"Boss's orders. If you keep trying to pay, she'll probably get agitated and start chattering at you, literally. It's a porcupine thing."

"I've noticed her teeth chattering a couple times. I didn't realize it was an instinctive response."

"Yeah, and she hates it. But it's out of her control, like all of our monster traits are. If you have a few minutes, I'd like to explain mine. I did a shit job in the alley the other day, and I don't like the way we left things."

"Neither do I," Elise says before laughing softly. "I suppose that's obvious, since I've come to your coffee shop every day since. You probably think I'm pathetic and desperate."

"I'd never think either of those things about you." I

tap my fingers on the edge of the table. "Do you mind if I sit?"

"Please do." Her head tilts as I slide onto the bench across from her. "I can see the imprint of your body on the cushion."

"My body's invisible, but it's still solid."

She leans forward, a wistful sigh floating from her lips. "I bet it is. I haven't forgotten our conversations."

My cock pushes against the front of my pants, eager to show her just how solid it is. That can't happen, yet I find myself resting my forearms on the table, getting closer than I should. "I wanted to call you. I should have, because you deserve the entire story, starting from the beginning, about how half the town turned into monsters."

"Oh, I know that part. Leroy told me about the scientist who made a toxic batch of punch for a community Halloween party."

"Leroy from The Sunnyside Motel?"

She nods. Sweetly. Innocently. "He's been really helpful since I got to town. And when I told him I've decided to move here, he said there's no rush for me to check out of the motel. He offered to let me keep my room for as long as I want, and he'll give me a reduced monthly rate that's equivalent to renting an apartment."

"You can't stay there." It's one of the rare times when I'm glad to be invisible, because she can't see my jaw clenching or the possessiveness in my gaze.

"Why not?"

"Because Leroy has ulterior motives. He's a player, and you're a beautiful, unattached woman."

"I don't feel unattached," she says, her eyes searching the place where my face should be. "I don't want to be unattached." She slides her hand across the table as if she means to touch me, but stops short. "I want to be with you, and I think you want that, too."

"My heart's already with you. It's never going to be anywhere else."

Lips that should be kissed breathless—something I'll never be able to do—curve into an achingly beautiful smile. "That's all I wanted to hear. It's all that matters."

"But it shouldn't be. You deserve someone who can give you everything. I'm not just invisible, Elise, I make things invisible. That's why I wear the metal-mesh gloves. To prevent contact."

"Has that happened? Have you touched someone and they became invisible?"

"No. I haven't had physical contact with anyone since the night I changed."

"What about the scientist who created the toxic punch?" she asks. "Does he think you'll make other people invisible if you touch them?"

I grunt a laugh. "That man accidentally turned half a town into a grab bag of monsters. I wouldn't trust him to hypothesize about the weather during a torrential downpour."

"Well, there's one way to know for sure. Take off your gloves and touch me. I'm not afraid of becoming invisible. I used to wish I were. It's a risk I'm willing to take."

"I'm not. Especially not with you. If my touch changes you, and you ever became ill or were injured, there'd be no way to properly assess your condition. I couldn't live with myself if something happened to you because of me. You're too important. You're the sunshine in every day of my life."

"That's beautiful."

"You're beautiful. Inside and out. You should be with someone who can give you all the things I can't."

"If it's my decision to make, then I've already made it. I want to be with you."

"Without seeing me? Without ever touching me? Is that going to be enough for you?"

"I see you, Roan. I've seen the most important parts of you for months now." She curls her delicate fingers over my gloved hand. "What about this? Do you feel safe touching like this?"

The blender noise behind the counter masks my groan. Even with a layer of steel mesh separating us, I can feel the warmth of her skin. The pressure of her touch is like a match strike, and my entire being is kindling. "Safe from harming you, yes."

"Then, we have options, if you want to try them."

"There's nothing I want more than to try every possible option with you."

The least subtle whooping imaginable rings through the coffee shop. My eavesdropping employee's stamp of approval.

"I'm taking the rest of the day off," I call over my shoulder. "Close the shop whenever you're ready to go home, Mel. And feel free to give people free coffee."

"Will do, boss!"

I take Elise's hand once we're out of the booth. It's been twenty long years since I held someone's hand, and the simple sensation—even without skin-to-skin contact—is fucking intoxicating. Even more so because it's Elise.

"Wait," she says, before we take a step. "Let me switch to your other side."

I don't have to ask why. The way she's angling her face tells me the reason for her request—she wants to put the scarred side of her face as far away as possible. I get it. She survived a brutal accident, and people weren't always kind about its physical toll on her skin. Those days are behind her. I'm in front of her, and she never needs to hide from me.

"You can't read my expression," I say, "but if you could, you'd know without a doubt that I think you're beautiful from all sides. If we're going to make this work, it's going to take honest communication and trust."

She tips her chin up, putting the scarred half of her face in full view. "I trust you."

Fuck, I want to kiss her. Since that's never going to happen, I gently squeeze her hand. "I'll always protect and cherish you." And love. But this isn't the place I want to tell her for the first time. "It's almost five. Can I take you out for dinner?"

"Or we go to your house and work up an appetite exploring our options." A deep-pink blush colors her cheeks. "Do you have another pair of those gloves?"

"I do," I say as we head for the coffee shop's door. Nobody can see the ear-to-ear grin on my face, but it's there. It never crossed my mind to think outside the box about a relationship. And I'm glad. Because I can't imagine exploring the options with anyone other than Elise.

Chapter Five

ELISE

"This is it," Roan says, opening the front door of a small white bungalow. One silver glove appears to be floating as he gestures for me to step inside. "My beautiful lady first."

"Thank you." I don't know if I'll ever look in the mirror and see beyond the scars, but when Roan tells me I'm beautiful, I *feel* beautiful.

Inside, he flips on the light. Beyond the small, open entryway is a living room. Metal blinds dress the windows. A metal-and-glass coffee table sits in front of a couch.

"Hey," I say, turning toward him, and wishing yet again I could see his face. "I assumed the room would look mostly empty, but I can see the couch. And at the coffee shop, the booth bench was still visible when you sat on it."

"Because they're both vinyl. Metal, glass, plastic, vinyl, varnished wood... Most non-porous materials don't react when I touch them."

"Then why not wear a vinyl apron and gloves, instead of the metal mesh? Ooh, or vinyl clothes?"

"Tried them. Too hot and sweaty."

Roan plus hot and sweaty sends a tingle rippling through me. Then the lightbulb goes on above my head. "What about latex? Does it react to your body chemistry?"

"No. I wear latex gloves when I'm working in the stockroom or office. But when I'm around people, I use the metal mesh because it's a thicker barrier. There's no chance they'll be compromised if I touch something sharp or hot."

"I don't think we have to worry about those things when we're alone together," I say, placing my palms on his apron, around what I estimate to be chest height. The fine mesh is still cool from our walk in the autumn air, but I can feel the warmth of his body beneath, along with his heartbeat.

He holds very still while I run my hands over the protected portion of his chest, then lower, over his stomach. He's broad, solid, and lean, exactly as I imagined.

My bravery from the coffee shop flickers back to life, and I skate my hands lower, to the hard ridge of his cock. It's long and pronounced, and I can't resist curling my fingers over it and rubbing up and down.

"Elise." His voice is tight and hoarse, as if he's barely holding it together.

I don't want him to hold it together. "Let's get some of those latex gloves and go to your bedroom."

His body tenses beneath my touch. "I want to. Fuck, do I want to." The unspoken *but* looms between us.

"I know you're worried that we'll be tempted to cross the line once we're in the moment, but—" I gasp as he cups my face in his gloved hands, then tips my chin up.

"I'm tempted now." The warmth of his breath tickles my lips. "It's already taking every drop of control I have not to kiss you."

Then do it. I bite my tongue to hold back the words I know would push him away. "Would it help if I forbid it?" I ask instead.

"Yes."

"Then kissing me is forbidden." *For now.* I shiver as he trails his fingers down my neck. It doesn't matter that it's not skin to-skin. He's touching me. He wants me. "And I promise not to kiss you, either," I say, giving his hard cock a gentle squeeze. "Because you're not the only one who's struggling with their self-control, you know."

"I don't know how I got lucky enough to find you." He takes a deep breath, releasing it slowly as he captures my hands. "Even if I could never touch you at all, having you here is the happiest time of my life."

"Mine, too."

Holding my hand, he leads me down a short hallway to a room with an open door. "I don't have a vinyl bed, so this room is going to look strange," he says, reaching inside to turn on the light.

I point at what appears to be a wrought-iron frame and rows of mattress pocket coils seeming to float in midair. "There's an actual bed there, right?"

Standing behind me, his deep chuckle slides into my ear like a delicious promise. "Yeah. A king-size mattress with cream-colored sheets and a dark-green duvet, even though neither of us can see them."

This is definitely going to take some getting used to. I move to the bed, then pat around on what appears to be nothingness, but is actually buttery soft bedding. "I guess you don't have to separate your lights from darks on laundry day."

"No," he says, chuckling. "Stains aren't a problem, either."

"So there *are* perks to invisibility." I shrug out of my heavy cardigan and toss it onto a hardback chair. "Okay, here goes!" Arms in front of me, I dive onto the bed I can't see. "Oh my God!" I squeal into the fluffy duvet, looking through the mattress while moving my arms and legs as if I'm making snow angels. "This is so wild."

Roan's full laughter booms from across the room. "Will you be angry if I call you cute?"

"Never," I say, switching to a seated position, then to a kneel. Heart pounding in my chest, I pull off my knit top and toss it onto the floor. "But I wouldn't mind if you use other adjectives, too."

He whistles under his breath when I unhook my bra and send it to join my top. "You're fucking gorgeous. How's that adjective?"

"Very good." The scarring on my right shoulder and arm is much less than my face, but it's still noticeable. I have no way to know if he's looking at any of it, but the tingly feeling spreading through my body makes me think he's watching me with desire. "I haven't been naked in front of anyone except medical professionals since my accident."

"I hate that people haven't appreciated you the way you deserve, but I'm not going to lie, I'm glad their stupidity worked in my favor."

"So am I. Even before the scars, I wasn't this comfortable with anyone." Is it because I can't see him? That may be part of it, but not the whole reason. There's something special between us. I've known it since the first day we exchanged messages. I shimmy to the edge of the bed, then off. "I've never been drawn to another person like I am to you."

He makes a rumbling, growly noise as I undo the button and zipper on my jeans, then push the denim down to my hips. "Stop."

I freeze instantly, the heat of embarrassment threatening to burn me to the ground.

"Wait for me to grab those gloves. I want to do the rest."

Relief rushes in, putting out one fire as a different flame ignites between my legs. "Then hurry and get them, and don't forget a pair for me, too."

"Be right back," he says, turning and disappearing from the room.

Physically, I see his gloves and apron moving. But I've been watching him all week, and as crazy as it sounds, I swear I'm starting to really see him. Not colors or features, and not an outline, exactly, but the shape of him. He's invisible, yes, but his body's mass changes how the air looks. Distorts it somehow.

Or maybe I'm so desperate to visually see him that my mind is playing tricks on me.

My hearing isn't working overtime, though. Once he's out of the room, he sounds like any man might, dropping his shoes in the hall, banging a cabinet door, treading the floor with lead-footed steps. A man in a hurry.

"I heard you giggling in here," he says, returning to the bedroom minus the silver gloves and apron. It explains some of the thudding—that metal-mesh apron must weigh a few pounds.

"You were making a lot of noise. Invisible or not, you'd be a terrible spy."

"I was very motivated to get back in here."

My attention is glued to the pair of latex gloves he's pulling on as he closes the distance between us.

He hands me a second pair, waits for me to put

them on, then takes my hands in his. "You're every-thing to me, Elise. Maybe that seems like too much, too soon, but it's true."

"It's true for me, too."

He releases my hands, then cups my face in his palms. "Say the word at any point and I'll stop."

"What's the word to make you *start?*"

His chuckle is a whisper of warmth over my face. A little squeak leaves my parted lips as he trails his fingers down my neck, along my shoulders, then over the swell of my breasts. I'm holding my breath by the time he reaches my nipples.

Cupping my breasts, he strums the hard peaks with his thumbs. "If I could put my mouth on you, I'd run my tongue all over your beautiful skin, then I'd pull each pretty nipple between my lips. Between my teeth. I'd suck and bite you until you were grabbing my head and begging me to make you come."

"I'm ready to beg now." My heart feels as if it's trying to beat its way out of my chest as he slides his hands lower, to my hips.

He works my jeans and panties down, removes my shoes, then rids me of the last of my clothing. "You are so fucking beautiful."

I shiver as he caresses every inch of my skin from my calves to my thighs. "Oh God," I whisper as he skims my pussy for the first time. And when he slides two fingers along my seam and settles the pads of his fingers against my clit, I have to grab hold of his wide, bare shoulders for support.

"Let's get you in a better position," he says, rising from his knees.

"That one was working pretty well in my opinion."

"I've barely started touching you, and you're already wobbly on your feet."

"But it's a good wobbly."

"It's a *great* wobbly." He cups my waist with his big hands, guiding me backward until my legs connect with the bed. "But I'd rather you didn't have to think about your balance while I'm making you come."

"Okay, I really can't argue with that."

"Glad to hear it," he says with a chuckle. "Hop up on the bed. I'd pick you up, but I don't want to accidentally make unprotected contact."

I do as I'm told, bracing myself in position by curling my hands over the edge of the bed. I can't take my eyes off the distorted air in front of me. From the location and position of his gloved hands, I know he's standing, and he's close. From the riot of awareness racing through me, I know he's looking at me. That he's hungry for me.

"I have a condom in my purse," I say, spreading my legs wider. "I bought them for this trip, for us. They're latex, so we could do more than touch with our hands…"

"Sweetheart, being careful so that I *only* touch you with my hands is going to be a challenge. There's no way I could be buried inside you without the rest of our bodies touching."

Need tightens in my core at the thought of his

weight pressing me into the mattress. "There has to be a way."

"Only if someone out there makes a full-body condom."

"Oh! We could make one!" I hop off the bed and plant my palms on his chest. It's a nice chest, muscular and solid, as is his stomach, when I slide my hands lower. "Not an actual body condom, but a body barrier."

"Keep going," he says, mapping every curve and divot he can carefully reach.

I'm not sure if he means my touch or my idea, but I'm giving him both. Because now that he's mine to explore, I need to feel all of him. "You might think it's too weird," I say, popping the button on his pants and lowering the zipper so I can wrap my fingers around his thick, rock-solid cock.

"I've dreamed about you for half a year. Now you're here, naked in my bedroom, stroking my dick. Bring on the weird. As long as it keeps you safe, I'll do anything with you."

"Including cut a cock hole in your shower curtain, or wrap my body in plastic wrap?"

His hands still. "You'd want that?"

"I want you. Any and every way we can make work," I say, following the column of his neck to his strong, bearded jaw. "I told you we'd have options."

He laughs and cups my face, tipping it upward as if to kiss me, though I know he won't take that risk.

"Sexy, smart, and incredibly creative. How did I get so lucky?"

"Well, you *did* tell me you're a giant leprechaun."

"So I did." He sweeps his thumb across my bottom lip, then releases me. "I'll be right back, my beautiful, perfect pot of gold."

I'm about to have the most unconventional sex of my life, the first sex I've had in a decade, and I'm not nervous at all. Because I trust him. And I'm utterly and completely in love with him.

At the sound of Roan's heavy-footed approach, I hurry to collect the condom from my purse. I'm facing away from the door when he enters the room, and laughter bursts from my lips when I turn toward him.

"A ghost with only one eye?" I ask as he advances on me with a white plastic sheet draped over his head.

"An invisible man with only one cock." He pulls the sheet off and tosses it onto the bed. "I love the sound of your laugh. The way your face and eyes light up when you do."

"Thank you."

"No, sweetheart. Thank you," he says, cupping my waist and holding me close enough to feel the warmth radiating from his body. "For answering my ad and getting to know me in a more real way than anyone else has. For bringing life to my existence."

"For breaking your primary rule, for refusing to accept your pigheadedness when you tried to scare me away..." I add, before I get swept away in emotion and tell him the depth of *my* feelings.

"Yeah, for those things, too." He gives my waistline a gentle squeeze before releasing me. "Now get your sexy ass on the bed, the way you were before. I barely got started, and I was nowhere near finished."

I add the condom package to the thin plastic sheet, and settle on the edge of the bed in front of him. There's a light *thud* as his knees hit the floor, then his hands are on my thighs, gently parting them. Goose bumps rise all over my body under his gentle, sensual touch. The closer he gets to my center, the faster my pulse races.

My hips have a mind of their own, tipping forward greedily the moment his fingers slide between my legs. I grab fistfuls of the duvet, because the more he rolls lazy circles over my clit, the more I want to grab him and pull him in. For a man who hasn't been with anyone in decades, he certainly knows his way around the female anatomy.

He slides two long, thick fingers inside me, groaning at my body's tight welcome, while working my clit with his other hand.

"Faster," I whisper, rocking against his fingers. "Oh God, yes, just like that..." I moan as he finds the perfect pressure and rhythm, sending me into a white-hot orgasmic spiral.

His husky growl is hot against my sensitive flesh. "I wanted to draw that out a lot longer."

"Sorry not sorry."

"Me either," he says, continuing to worship me with his skillful fingers until my body is shamelessly angling to get more. "Also not sorry I'm going to do it again."

The need for release tugs tighter with every orbit of his fingers over my clit. "I want you inside me the next time." I pick up the condom package and hold it between us, biting my lip when he doesn't take it immediately. "We'll be careful. Like you just were when you were touching me."

He exhales, long and low, then takes the packet from my hand. "I can't help thinking this isn't fair to you. Making love with a plastic sheet between us? That wasn't what you had in mind when you bought these condoms."

"I only had one thing in mind and it hasn't changed." I reach out until I find his face, then run my fingers along the line of his brows. "I want to be with you."

"And I only want to be with you," he says, catching one of my hands and pressing a kiss to the Venus mount of my palm.

One day, I'll feel his lips on my skin. I know it with every tingling molecule in my body. I know it in my heart and soul. Until then, I'm happy about what we have.

He keeps ahold of my hands, settling them on the front of his open pants once he's standing. "Take my cock out, sweetheart."

I shove his pants and boxer briefs out of the way, then slide my fist up and down his thick, tall cock. He's big. Really big. And I can't wait to feel every inch of him inside me.

"Fuck, that's good. So good, but I need to be buried deep in your beautiful body."

"Finally," I say, releasing him so I can move up onto the bed. "I've only been waiting six months for this."

His chuckle mixes with the sound of fabric rustling. Then he tears into the condom package, tosses it aside, and rolls the latex down his cock—which, now that I can see it, looks even bigger than it felt in my hand. *Hubba hubba*.

"I've been waiting my whole life," he says, the bed shifting beneath his weight.

"Do you mean—" Nope, can't bite my tongue on this one. I need to know. "Are you a virgin?"

"No. But the sex I had as an eighteen-year-old was about raging hormones. It was sex just for the sake of sex. I wasn't in love then."

My breath catches at the words, my hopeful heart galloping in my chest.

"Come here," he says, holding out his hands after settling the sheet over his broad, solid body. He holds me steady as I straddle his hips, positioning myself above his tall, hard cock. "I want you more than I've ever wanted anyone. Not because it's been twenty years, or because it's going to feel fucking amazing to be inside you. Because I'm in love with you."

"I love you, too," I say softly, blinking back the happy

tears welling in my eyes. I lean forward, nearly giving in to my urge to kiss him. I don't care if I become invisible—I just want to be with him. Completely. In all the ways.

I also want to make him happy in every way possible, so I pull back, flatten my palms on his chest, and sink onto his cock. "Oh God..." I moan as his thick girth stretches me.

"Elise." My name comes out on a growl. He grips me tight, pulling me down, spreading me open, filling me to the hilt. "So fucking good."

Unable to speak, I bite my lip and nod. I grab his pecs and brace myself. The rustle of plastic and our ragged breathing fills the room as I ride him, hard and fast, loving the hungry groans rumbling beneath my palms. He's mine, and I'm his.

Heat rips through me, and I grind against his pelvis, panting as the pressure builds in my clit and beneath his touch. *"Roan..."* is all I get out before sensation steals my ability to do anything other than writhe and grind on him as I come completely undone.

Roan's deep grunts join my breathy moans. He thrusts into me once more, then his body jerks and shudders as his cock pulses deep inside me. "Fuck..."

I pancake onto his heaving chest, digging my chin into his sternum as I look up to the face I can't see, but I know without a doubt has a smile to match mine. "Aren't you glad we opted for the options?"

His body shakes with silent laughter, dislodging me from my new favorite option. "Very glad."

"Put your arm above your head," I say, arranging

the plastic sheet so I can snuggle against his side. "*I'm glad nobody else you've met thought of the options before me.*"

"There hasn't been anyone else. Only you."

I sigh as he strokes my hair. "That feels nice."

"You have beautiful hair. I bet it's as soft as silk."

I want to tell him to take his glove off and touch it, but the words dissolve into a contented purr before they make it off my tongue. I mumble something unintelligible instead, and his big, warm chest rumbles beneath my ear. Weight tugs my eyelids closed, and try as I might, I can't fight the relaxation that washes over me.

"Goodnight, sweetheart," he says softly. Then, "I love you," right before the sandman steals me away.

Chapter Six

ROAN

She's gone when I wake up. Since she had to walk past me to get to the front door, she either has a much better stealth mode than mine, or she was just highly motivated to get away without talking to me.

She hasn't texted and didn't leave a note, so it has to the second option. Morning-after regret? I fucking hope not. Maybe she's upset that she woke up alone. I didn't have another option. She was so beautiful and vulnerable when she fell asleep at my side. The sound of her breathing, the smell of her hair, the soft noises she makes in her sleep...

I didn't want to leave her. But if I'd stayed in bed, I would've drifted off, too. I would've ended up wrapped around her, skin to skin. Not a chance I can take with her. There are no safe options for sleeping together in the literal sense.

I need to explain that. Tell her I spent the night on the couch because I love her, and for no other reason. I'm due at work in an hour, but talking to Elise is top priority, and not something I want to do over the phone. It has to be face to face. Crazy how much my outlook—hell, every aspect of my life—has changed.

After a quick text to Melinda to arrange opening coverage for Lucky Beans, I hop in the car and head for The Sunnyside Motel. Elise's car is parked in front of a row of numbered rooms, but I don't know which is hers. Shit. I've known Leroy Shortt since high school. We both played football, and even though we were on the same team, there was always rivalry between us. Competing for the cutest girls in school will do that.

We're not competing for Elise—she came to Screaming Woods to be with me. Just because I know it doesn't mean Leroy does, or that he'll accept it. Hell, I probably wouldn't in his position. Elise is a woman worth fighting for.

The motel's office door is propped open, allowing me to enter undetected. I've built my life around being ethical with my transparency, but I don't call out a hello when I reach the desk. I'll take every bit of upper hand I can get with Leroy. And if I scare him a little... that won't hurt, either.

I've been in this building before, so I skirt the desk and head down the short hall to Leroy's office, stopping dead in my tracks when I reach the open door. Leroy and Elise are in front of a desk, standing too fucking close together and looking too damn friendly to be discussing a room rental rate.

"I don't think Roan will be as agreeable about this as you want, but what's mine is yours," Leroy says, taking her hand. Her bare hand. "Whenever you're ready, Elise, I'll provide what you need."

"Thank you."

His long, forked tongue darts out when she places a kiss on his scaly cheek. Then he pulls her into a hug, staring through me with his big, unblinking eyes. The bastard knows I'm here. The snake can smell me.

"Roan?" Elise extricates herself from Leroy's arms and turns toward me. *She* can't scent me. She can't see me, either. It's physically impossible, yet I swear she's looking *at* me, not through me. She doesn't have any monsterly abilities, but she knows I'm here. "I was just about to call you and ask when you could stop by."

"And now you don't have to call."

Her beautiful face is beaming as she looks toward Leroy. "Can we do it now? Are you ready?"

Did I dream everything from last night? Or was fucking the invisible man just some kink to unlock, and now she's moving on to Leroy?

"Ready when you are," Leroy says, then, "I'll give you a minute alone to tell him."

Tightly balled fists at my sides, I step aside so Leroy can leave. I've spent two decades growing into a calm, responsible man, but in this moment, my genetically ingrained Irish fight demands I punch Leroy's fangs down his damn throat.

"Tell me what?" I ask as she closes the distance between us. "And how did you know I was here, or where I'm standing now?"

"I could feel your eyes on me. And I know you're going to tell me it's impossible, but I can see you."

"You're right, it's impossible." I can't even see myself in the mirror. God knows I've tried.

"Only, it's not," she says, shaking her head. "I can't see the surface of you. Not the color of your eyes or hair. But I can see the shape of you. You're invisible, but you're solid—*very solid*—and mass takes the place of air. I see you."

"No one else ever has. It's wishful thinking."

"Maybe my eyesight is tuned differently. Or maybe I'm meant to be the only person who sees you, just like you're the only one who sees me."

"Leroy sure seems able to see you," I say with a grunt.

Her delicate eyebrows knit together at the bridge of her nose. "Looking at someone and seeing them are different things."

Telling her she's right won't change anything. I cross my arms over my chest. A defensive posture, though there's no protecting my heart from what's about to happen. "What do you want to tell me?"

"That you were wrong."

"Yeah, I got that already." I exhale as the lips I'd

give anything to kiss curve downward. "Say what you need to say, and I'll get out of your way."

"Get out of my way? What does that mean?"

Fuck. "It means I saw you and Leroy having the kind of cozy, close-contact moment you and I can never have. I'm invisible, not blind. You want the things I can't give you, and you should. You deserve to have everything, without limits and barriers, whether it's with Leroy or someone else."

"You're... jealous? After everything we said and shared last night?"

"Just being realistic." I curse under my breath when she mimics my posture while drilling me with an I-call-bullshit gaze. "Yes, I'm jealous. So fucking jealous, I'd be green if I wasn't invisible."

"I'd love you if you were green. I love you regardless of shape, size, color, or lack thereof. You saw friendship and gratitude. That's all I'll ever want to have with Leroy, or with anyone except you."

"Elise—"

"Are we ready for Screaming Woods' next science experiment?" Leroy robs me of the opportunity to grovel at Elise's feet when he walks into the room carrying a cardboard box with tiny ventilation holes. His snake-eyed gaze shifts back and forth between us. "Should I come back?"

"No. Roan can finish what he was about to say afterward. It'll be even better then."

"All right, let's get on with the big moment," Leroy says, opening the box after setting it on the desk. "I haven't had breakfast yet, and these little fellas are making me hungry."

"What's going on?" I ask, following Elise to the desk.

"When I woke up alone in your bed this morning, I thought you'd gone to the coffee shop already. I was on my way out when I heard you snort—that's when I realized you were asleep on the couch."

"I had to, Elise. I couldn't risk touching you while I was sleeping."

"I know why you slept there." Her voice is like a soft touch. "I love how committed and protective you are. But after what I saw, I think you're wrong about the risk."

"What did you see?"

"You snorted because there was a spider on you. A pretty gross one, I'm sorry to tell you, making its way casually across your face."

Instinctively, I swipe both palms over my nose and cheeks. "How do you know it was my face? Wait—do I even want to know?"

Her pretty features scrunch up as she cringes. "Probably not."

Fuck, I have to know. "Did it crawl into my mouth? Did I eat a spider in my sleep?"

"It did, but you didn't eat it. You spat it onto the floor."

"What a waste," Leroy says, doing the snake equivalent of licking his lips.

"The spider was black, Roan. Fully black, not invisible, after prolonged direct contact with your skin."

The impact of her words nearly takes me out at the knees. I grab the back of the closest chair for support, grimacing as the upholstery immediately becomes invisible. "Shit. Sorry, Leroy. I owe you a new chair."

"No worries." His tongue darts out as he motions me over. "You're not as afraid of mice as you are of spiders, are you?"

"I'm not afraid of spiders. I just don't want to eat them."

"To each their own," he says, smiling his snaky smile. "I find them to be a light, spicy snack. Not as filling as mice, obviously. Go ahead." He tips the box toward me. "Pick one up. Let's see if Elise's theory is correct."

"Theory?" I ask, looking at her.

"That your physiology doesn't affect living things, only porous, inanimate objects. I know you wouldn't be willing to test my theory on another animal, but these mice aren't long for this world anyway. They're Leroy's breakfast, whether they're white, gray, or invisible."

"And I'm quite hungry, so if you could get on with the experiment, and try not to agitate them too much while you're handling them. Changes their flavor, all the way down."

I've accepted and catered to our town's monsterly needs for twenty years, but the knowledge that Leroy swallows mice whole is enough to turn *my* stomach.

"Please," Elise says, getting as close to me as possible without actually touching. "Nothing between us will change if I'm wrong. We'll still be together, with options. Lots of them, because I'm discovering a creative side I didn't know I had."

I chuckle as my cock rises to attention. It loves Elise's creativity. I love everything about her, including her determination and optimism.

"And if I'm right, well..." Her voice is softer, vulnerable. "You'll know that you can be with anyone you want."

"That's you, sweetheart. Only you. Always." I've made a lot of wishes over the years, but I've never wanted one to come true more than when I dip my hands into the box and scoop up a small gray mouse.

The three of us watch that mouse in my hands for what feels like an eternity. And we *can* watch it, because it doesn't turn invisible. It doesn't change at all. Not even a little.

I'm still staring at the mouse when I feel Elise's hand curl over my wrist. Skin on skin. Every wish comes true with that one simple touch.

"Let's go to your house," she says, her beautiful eyes glassy as she smiles at me.

"Not to my house, sweetheart." I pass off the mouse, then cup her soft face in my hands, and brush my lips across hers for the first of a lifetime of kisses. "Let's go home."

ROAN

Having spent two decades keeping a low profile, it shocked everyone when we announced the location of our wedding—town square. If there's one thing Screaming Woods likes, it's a party. Showing the world how much I love Elise deserves the biggest celebration possible. The best way to do that? An open invitation.

The faces of our out-of-town guests dot the rows of white chairs. Beyond them, the standing-room area is packed with as many local monsters as the space can accommodate. When *If I Never Knew You* fills the spring air, and a fairytale-style carriage pulls up to the end of the aisle, I don't see anyone in attendance. Only my beautiful bride as she steps out of the coach.

Sunlight bounces off her white dress, surrounding her like a magical aura. She's so damn beautiful. The biggest smile I've ever seen bursts across her pretty face. Then she gathers the full skirt of her princess wedding gown in her hands and runs toward me.

"Your tuxedo!" she says as she reaches me. "It's amazing. I love it." She splays her palms on my chest, her bright eyes wide while she examines the fine-nylon mesh our neighborhood tailor used to create my three-piece suit and tie. "You didn't tell me you were having an invisible-proof tuxedo made."

"Because it's bad luck to see the groom's suit before the wedding."

"That's not how the superstition goes," she says, laughing and tugging my lapels.

"I thought you'd like to have pictures where you don't look abandoned on your wedding day."

She giggles, leans in carefully and kisses me. "I love you so much. Thank you for the wonderful surprise."

Screaming Woods' resident pastor, who also happens to be a faun, clears his throat to get our attention. "Shall we get started?"

"Definitely," I say, taking Elise's hands in mine. "You take my breath away, sweetheart. Today and every day."

Silence falls over our community of guests as the pastor begins the ceremony. I want time to slow down so I can savor every second of this day. I also can't wait for it to be over, so I can be alone with the love of my life. My beautiful, smart, sexy wife.

ROAN

"Finally," Elise says when I unlock our front door. "It was a wonderful day, the best day, but I'm happy it's over so I can have my husband's full attention."

I chuckle as I follow her through the house. We both know I didn't take my eyes—or hands—off her unless circumstances required it. Since discovering I could touch her, I've spent every available minute doing just that. After my casually placed bare hand on the small of her back rendered her seemingly topless in Il Diablo, though, I'm very careful in public. Thank goodness the small Italian restaurant wasn't at capacity that night.

To be on the safe side today, I wore latex gloves. I didn't want an accidental touch leaving my bride naked in front of hundreds of people. Her body is for my eyes only. And my eyes need to see every sexy inch.

"Want help with your zipper before I take off my gloves?" I ask, moving in close behind her in the bedroom. Tempted as I am to wrap my arms around her, I resist. I know she'd be disappointed if her beautiful gown disappeared.

"Yes, please." She tilts her head and lifts the fall of

loose curls in her hands, giving me the perfect opportunity to kiss her slender neck.

"You smell good enough to eat, Mrs. Byrne."

"*Mmm...* I was hoping you'd have room for dessert when we got home."

Lowering the zipper should be a utilitarian action, but my cock gets harder with every descending inch. "You're free," I say, stepping back to a safe distance. Only it's not, because the moment the fancy white fabric pools at her feet, I'm on fire for her. "Jesus, you're beautiful. You'd better take those off." I gesture at the pale-pink bra and panties. "Because I'd like to see them on you again, but I'm two damn seconds away from putting my hands all over you."

"You'd better take those off." There's a huge smile on her face as she does a terrible job of mimicking me while pointing at everything I'm wearing. "Because I wanted you naked and inside me two damn seconds ago."

I laugh while getting the fuck out of the most uncomfortable clothes in the world. Stuff I'd wear all day, every day, if she wanted me to. Once I'm naked, I'm invisible—almost. I spin my wedding band on its forever home on my left hand. "Now you'll always be able to see me."

"I always could."

I'm in her space in one stride. I scoop her into my arms, kiss her breathless as I carry her to our bed. "I love you so fucking much."

"Show me," she says, pulling her bottom lip between her teeth.

I lay her out on the bed and cover her with my body. "Too heavy?" I already know the answer. I just want to hear it.

"I love your weight on me, the feeling of your big, warm body touching every inch of me."

Cue taken. I nudge her legs apart and notch my cock against her pussy, sliding into her tight, wet heat as I seal my mouth over hers. I swallow her moan, then every one after it as I stroke and grind, deep and hard.

She breaks the kiss, moaning my name against my lips as her pussy squeezes my cock.

Buried deep, I rock against her, pushing her into a second wave of climax. When she's wrung out and panting, I taste her lips one more time, then kiss my way down her body.

Sensitive from coming around my cock, she tries wriggling away when I settle between her thighs and bury my face in her pussy.

I sling one arm over her body with enough pressure to hold her in place. Her hard nipples are ripe for the plucking, and that's exactly what I do. Lightly at first, increasing the pressure of my pinches with each sweep of my tongue through her pussy.

"Oh God," she moans, pushing her fingers through my hair. "More... harder..."

I suck her clit between my lips, between my teeth, working her tender bud with my tongue until heat prickles over my scalp from her nails. The best fucking pain in the world. I growl against her pussy as she bucks beneath me, arching off the bed and coming on my tongue.

"I need you inside me." Her breathless voice is barely a whisper.

I take one last taste of my favorite dessert, then move up her body, burying myself to the balls as I kiss her sweet lips. I'm too far gone to last long, but when I go, I'm taking her with me. I hitch one of her legs up, opening her wider so I can stroke her G-spot with every thrust.

"Roan," she whimpers against my mouth, grabbing my back, my butt.

Fire licks at the base of my cock. Not yet. Not fucking yet.

Her body tightens beneath mine, then the bowstring snaps. "Oh God..." She pulls me impossibly deeper, grinding against me as her pussy squeezes me to perfection.

"Elise, fuck, *fuuuck*..." Arms wrapped around her, I raise her hips up and fill her with everything I have. "I love you, sweetheart. Only you. Forever and always."

"What if I told you it might be possible for you to love another person, too?" Her voice is so quiet, I almost don't hear the question. *Almost.*

My pulse takes off like a rocket, and I push up on my arms to look into my beautiful wife's eyes. "What are you saying?"

"My doctor friend who took your samples when he

was in town for our engagement party said all the tests he ran came back without anomalies."

The guy was a pro, I'll give him that. Didn't look at anyone in town like a freak. Didn't have any trouble finding a vein on my invisible arm. And he didn't tell Elise that I damn near passed out when the vial started to fill with my definitely not-invisible blood.

"No anomalies in any of the tests?" Because blood wasn't the only sample I sent with the good doctor that day.

"Everything was within normal, healthy parameters." She wraps her arms around my neck, the prettiest blush tinting her cheeks as she strokes my hair. "He thinks your invisibility is similar to scar tissue. Cells that have been damaged at surface level. He said there's no evidence to support concerns about genetic transference."

"Does that mean what I think it means?"

Her silky hair moves like gentle lapping waves as she nods. "It means we could be the Byrne family one day, if you want that."

"If I want that?" I drop a kiss on her lips before springing from the bed. I'm like a bull in a china shop as I barrel toward the bathroom. A minute later, I'm back in our room, in our bed, with her birth-control pills in my hand.

Her eyes go wide as saucers when I crumple the small foil blister package in my fist, then toss it into the wastebasket.

I skim my palms over her body, taking extra time

to slide them over her abdomen. Flat now, but not for long. "I want a family with you," I say, settling on top of her and sliding into her perfect warm pussy with one deep thrust. Then another, and another. I fuse our mouths together, groaning when she sucks my tongue as deep as she can take it.

Her breathy moan vibrates against my lips. "God, yes... *yes...*"

Heady, deep-seated need roars inside me as she comes. The need to claim. To provide. "Fuck, I love you," I growl, rutting on her until I come so deep inside her, I can't feel where I end and she begins. The way it always is with her. The way it has been since the first time, and will be every day, for the rest of our lives.

**Turn the page
to read Leroy's story in
*Snake Believe!***

Snake Believe

Monster Between The Sheets

KARLA DOYLE

CORA

Sent to Screaming Woods to write a magazine piece on its resident monsters, I'm ready to meet hairy beasts, ogres, vampires... Heck, I even have an interview scheduled with an actual invisible man. What I'm not prepared for? A snake man. I'm terrified of snakes. Now I'll have to talk to a man-sized one on a daily basis, because he owns the motel where I'm staying and there are no vacancies elsewhere in town.

Once the initial shock of coming face to face with a walking, talking snake passes, I start to see Leroy for the man beneath the monster exterior. And the more I get to know my snake man, the more I realize my biggest fear would be losing him.

LEROY

At nineteen, I unknowingly drank the poisoned party punch that turned many of Screaming Woods' residents into monsters. My future as a human vanished when I became a snake man. Twenty-plus years later, I wouldn't change back if I could. I have the best of both species in me. My new anatomy has definite advantages, and because of *them*, I'm frequently propositioned. But that's not the kind of proposal I seek.

I'm the loneliest snake in town until the day Cora walks into the motel I own—and promptly faints at the sight of me. The lovely magazine reporter is only in town to interview monsters for an article, but I know from the first day that I won't want to say goodbye to her. My charms have never failed me before, but I'm a one-hundred-and-eighty-pound embodiment of her biggest fear.

That won't stop me from trying. Anything is possible in Screaming Woods.

Chapter One

CORA

As the "fluff" girl for a popular online magazine, I write about topics that get quick clicks. Fashion, hair, and makeup trends. Dating dos and don'ts. Tips to improve your sex life. All things I have zero expertise in, because I rarely leave the snug safety of my one-bedroom apartment. My wardrobe consists of clothing designed for sloth-level comfort, it's been over a year since I set foot in a hair salon, and the closest thing to makeup I own is a cherry ChapStick. As for dating and sex tips... Let's just say, I'm the *last* person who should be giving recommendations.

Real-life me is about as cool as an unplugged refrigerator. Based on my articles' clicks and the affiliate earnings from the products I endorse, my online persona is hot as city pavement in summertime. So much so, my boss asked me to write a piece for the front page. A legit piece of journalism with actual interviews. My first opportunity to flex the degree I busted my butt to earn.

Of course I jumped at the offer. I blurted a yes as soon as my boss said he had a "monster of an opportunity" for me. In hindsight, I should've listened a longer. Then I would've known he meant the words literally.

Would I have said yes anyway, even if I'd known everything this assignment would entail? Abso-freak-ing-lutely, with emphasis on the freak part, based on the subject material. Turning down the chance to see my byline on the front page would be crazy. This could be my shot at something bigger than the *Trending* page—not that there's anything wrong with that chunk of real estate. *Trending* has paid the rent and kept the Uber Eats flowing to my door regularly. I have no regrets. But I also wouldn't be sad to move on.

I'm up for the assignment, even though it required me to put on pants with a zipper instead of an elastic waistband, and heeled leather boots instead of slippers with terrycloth-covered memory-foam insoles. My usual messy bun is on hiatus, replaced by a freshly coiffed style that brushes my shoulders. I'm even wearing real makeup—okay, just mascara, but still—and yes, it is the brand I promised would change my readers' lives in last month's column.

And you know what? I *do* feel like my life is about to change. Cosmetics and clothing don't get credit for the fluttery feeling in my stomach, though. This sensation is bigger than shining up my exterior. I'm at a turning point. *The* turning point. This is where I pivot.

First, I need to write the article that requires leaving my apartment for something other than curbside grocery pickup or a drive-thru run to meet my caffeine quota. I tried convincing my boss that I could do this piece remotely. I've proven myself with three years of pajama-powered, super-clickable content. Travel was mandatory for this gig, and not by my editor's choice.

Turns out, he didn't pluck this concept from his brain or borrow it from a competitor. This piece is by request. The mayor of Screaming Woods reached out to the magazine, looking for some positive spin on the town in return for what will undoubtedly be extremely clickable content. Now that Screaming Woods' two-decades-long secret is out in the open, they'd rather not have visitors armed with wooden stakes, silver bullets, and pitchforks. They want the world to understand that monsters are people, too.

That's the story. Certainly not one I ever imagined writing, but when the universe drops gold in your lap, you grab that nugget and run to the bank with it. Or take a two-hour flight followed by an ass-numbing drive with it, in this case. But I'm here now. Ready to spin Screaming Woods' monsters into my personal gold.

The town unfolds around me as I drive. At a glance, there's nothing unusual. Same blue sky, white clouds, green grass you'd find pretty much anywhere. The trees, buildings, cars... everything's normal. Until I spot my first monster.

At least seven-feet tall with dark fur, he has insanely broad shoulders, glowing red eyes, and a set of horns that'd make even the biggest elk jealous. The man—I should call him a man, right?—is walking his dog. A small, fluffy dog with a yellow bow wrapped around a tiny ponytail atop its head. Talk about opposites. The monster man must feel me gawking, because he turns his head at the exact moment I pass. Meeting my gaze, he smiles—at least I think that's a smile, though the rows of jagged teeth are menacing— and raises one hand to wave.

Okeydokey, shit is officially real. I quickly return the gesture before focusing on the road ahead. When I accepted this assignment, I had to sign a contract stating I understand that all the town's monsters were once human, and therefore, will be treated as such. No problem there. Journalists don't have bias. Not the good ones, anyway, and I'm great at my job. Besides, I've never been afraid of monsters. Not in books, TV, or movies. I'm the perfect candidate for this opportunity —aside from the leaving my apartment and having face-to-face interactions part.

By the time I arrive at the small motel where the town's administration has reserved me a room, I've seen monsters with horns, wings, fur, tails, and hooves. They didn't all randomly wave at me like the first one, but aside from their appearances, they seemed like normal people going about their lives. Zero scariness factor. I understand the mayor's concerns for the reputation and safety of Screaming Woods and its citizens, but I can't imagine anyone being fearful here. Any niggling concerns I had when I committed to delivering a positive article are gone. This piece is practically going to write itself.

I park my rental car, collect my bags from the trunk, then head into the main office of the cheery, charming building. The front desk is vacant—or is it? One of the monsters I'm scheduled to interview is an invisible man who owns a coffee shop downtown, but maybe he's not the only one.

"Hello?" I ask, shaking my head when silence ensues. Of course nobody answers, because I'm alone in the room. An invisible man would've greeted me when I walked in, obviously. Plus, I'd see his clothes. In town less than five minutes and already, my mind is in monster overdrive.

I step to the counter and tap the classic silver bell sitting on the desk, then pull out my phone to appear busy and nonchalant. Eager as I am to get settled in, I don't want to seem pushy or impatient. Peopling isn't my strong suit, even in familiar situations. Peopling with monsters takes it to a whole other level.

"Be right with you," a man calls from down a short hall.

I lean over the counter, ready to assure the owner

of the smooth voice that there's no need to rush, but all that comes out of my mouth is a strangled little sputter. Forming words is impossible now that he's walking toward me.

He's just a man. He's just a man.

No matter how many times I internally say the words, my mind refuses to believe them. I'm not afraid of monsters, but I am afraid of snakes.

"Welcome to The Sunnyside Motel," he says once he's behind the check-in desk.

Nope, I can't do it. I feel my mouth opening and closing, but nothing's coming out. And I'm shaking. Head-to-toe trembling.

"You must be Ms. Ravin, the journalist from the magazine."

I manage a small nod, then he—smiles? I think? It's hard to tell because his mouth is wide and almost lipless. Every inch of visible skin is green and scaly, and he stares at me with unblinking yellow eyes.

No screaming. No running. He's just a—

Before I can mentally complete the sentence, a long, black, forked tongue slithers out of his mouth. Only for a moment, but that's all it takes for my knees to buckle and the world to go dark.

LEROY

For a small woman, she made one hell of a thud when she dropped. I should've seen it coming. Every drop of color drained from her complexion when I walked into the room. Then there was the speechless fish-gaping. She's not from Screaming Woods, but she knows it's a town full of monsters. That's why she's here. And, as monsters go, I'm not the scariest one around. If she faints at the sight of me, she might as well skip check-in and go back to wherever she came from. That's a suggestion for later. Making sure she's okay is my first priority.

"Ms. Ravin..." Given her extreme response to my appearance, I shouldn't be the first thing she sees when she opens her eyes, but there's no one to take my place. Aside from the cleaning staffer who left several hours ago, I run the motel alone during the day. One person is enough with only six units to rent.

A soft groan passes through her parted lips, and she turns her head side to side on the folded sweater I slipped beneath it.

"Ms. Ravin, my name is Leroy, I'm the owner of this motel," I say as her eyelids flutter. "I'm the man who spoke to you before you fainted. You went down quite hard, so don't sit up too quickly."

No worries about that. Her body stiffens, and she clamps her arms over her chest. Rather than open her eyes, she pinches them closed tighter.

It's been over twenty years since the fateful night I

morphed in to a snake man, and nearly as long since somebody reacted to me so dramatically. If this woman wasn't an invited guest of the mayor, I'd... well, I don't know what I'd do. Not be rude, that's never been my style, even as a young human male.

I rise from my crouched position, then put distance between us. "I'm standing behind the counter now, Ms. Ravin. It doesn't appear that you're bleeding, but you have a large goose egg on the back of your head, so I advise you to take your time sitting up."

"Would you—" She exhales, the action deflating the rigidity of her form. Even in her supine position, her shoulders seem to slump. "Never mind."

"Would I what? I can't guarantee I'll accommodate your request, but neither of us will know until you make it."

"Turn around." The words are barely a whisper, yet they're unmistakable.

This woman is in *my* hometown, in *my* place of business, and she has the audacity to ask me to spare her the discomfort of viewing my face?

"It's not you, it's me," she says softly. "I—" Wrinkles form at the bridge of her nose, then she sighs. A defeated sound, as if she had all her money on red and the ball dropped on black. "I'm terrified of snakes."

"Then I'd say we have an 'it's me *and* it's you' problem, Ms. Ravin."

"I'm so sorry." She claps both hands over her face. "I shouldn't have asked you to turn around. That was incredibly rude and insensitive of me. I'm a hot mess in more ways than I can count, but I'm not usually an asshole. This is a total *me* issue. I'll make sure you're still paid the full amount for my stay, but it's probably best if I find another hotel, so I don't treat you horribly again." She shifts onto her side so she's facing away from me, groaning as she sits up. "God, this is the worst hangover ever."

Cute. Humor is a good sign. "Can I get you some water? I'll roll it across the floor for you. No direct contact required."

"No, I'm fine." Clearly interpreting the comment as a dig instead of a genuine offer, she hurries to stand— a movement that her body rejects. "Sorry, I want to get out of your way, I just need the room to stop spinning first," she says, plunking onto her ass.

It's a nice ass, even in this position. Since I know she won't turn around and catch me staring, I go right ahead and look my fill. I'm an appreciator of the female form in all variations, but her shape is my favorite—a curvy silhouette that begs to be traced. I'm a sucker for a cuppable waist and grippable hips. So much so, I have to rub my palms against my pants to calm the itch to touch her.

"You're not in my way," I say. "And the offer of a drink was sincere."

"Well...thank you. I'm fine, really." She touches the back of her head tenderly. "You weren't kidding about the goose egg."

"I never kid about eggs." The small joke earns me a soft laugh, and the sound gives me a spark I'm an idiot to feel. "Fortunately, you stumbled over your bags on the way down. If it'd been a direct drop, you'd likely be leaving on a gurney." There's no reason for me to feel warmth toward this woman, but the thought that she could've been seriously injured twists me up. "Take a few minutes to regroup while I make some calls to find you another room. Once that's taken care of, I'll arrange for a non-snaky taxi driver to get you there safely. Sound good?"

"It sounds like a lot more than I deserve after treating you the way I have. I really am sorry."

"Don't worry about it. I know you didn't walk in here intending to faint in fear at the sight of my face."

She groans again, this one sounding pained strictly with embarrassment. "Are you sure you want to help me?"

"One hundred percent," I say, pulling up the number of the nearest B&B.

"Thank you for being so kind and understanding."

"No thanks necessary. I'm only a monster on the outside."

"Oh. Of course. You know about the article." Her hair moves like soft brown waves while she nods. "Just for the record, I take full responsibility for this mess. I know I'm the problem. I'm only going to write good things about you and your motel; you don't have to worry about that. If that's why you're helping me find another place to stay—"

"It's not, Ms. Ravin."

"Okay, and...call me Cora. Or if that's too personal,

given the circumstances, then Miss Benton will do. That's my real name. Ravin is a pseudonym for the magazine. The owner likes all the writers to have 'cool' names," she says, complete with air quotes.

Just like that, the urge to smooth my hands over her curves returns. The *Miss* prefix doesn't guarantee she's single, but it improves the odds. Not that her relationship status matters. She finds me repulsive. Can't even look at me. When she walks out of here, I'll never see her again, because I'm the last person on earth she'd want to lay eyes on, let alone other body parts.

"Sit tight while I make some calls, Miss Benton."

"Will do," she says quietly, tucking her chin downward.

I'd like to think that's regret in her voice, in her posture. I'd like to, but I'm smarter than that now. Wanting something doesn't make it real. Not twenty-plus years ago, when I prayed every damn day for a way to change back from a snake to a regular man. Nor the times I believed I was at the beginning of a relationship, then realized that the woman was only interested in the pleasure my snake anatomy can provide.

The best thing I can do for both of us is to find Cora somewhere to go. Then do what she's doing right now—never turn around to look back.

Chapter Two

CORA

The dizziness has worn off by the time Leroy ends another call with, "Thanks for checking." This time, though, he doesn't immediately tap the next phone number. That can't be a good sign.

"No luck yet?" I ask from my embarrassing position, sitting on the floor in the middle of his lobby area. Thank goodness nobody else has come in since I lost my shit.

"I'm afraid it's worse than that, Miss Benton. There are no vacancies."

That can't be possible. Maybe he's only calling the nicest places, or is trying to stay within the same budget as my reservation here. "I'm not picky. I can stay anywhere. Five stars, one star, bed-and-breakfast, luxury suite... Heck, it can be a roach motel."

"Got it. Roach motel—good. Immaculate, well-appointed motel owned by a snake—bad."

"I didn't mean it that way." I pinch my eyes closed, but really, it's my mouth I should keep sealed. This is why I should only be allowed to work from the safety and seclusion of my apartment. Live, in-person communication always gets me in trouble, and this is definitely the worst time ever. I'm being a horrible person, plain and simple, and I hate it. "You have a cute motel and you're being so nice... This is all me. I had a terrible experience with snakes when I was young, and now I'm just—" I shudder at the memory of that day in the field with my older brothers and the rattlesnake. "It was a long time ago, and I'm overreacting. I just need a few minutes to turn off my brain."

Behind me, he exhales, long and slow. "I understand. Everyone's fears are different, and unfortunately, I'm yours."

"You're being way more understanding than I deserve."

"Would you do the same if our positions were reversed?"

"Absolutely," I say without having to give it any thought. I'd probably have a bag over my head already, to put him at ease.

"Then don't give it another thought. As for the vacancies, there are literally none of any level or variety in Screaming Woods. I also checked availability in the nearest town, but no luck on that front, either. There is a campground, if you'd like me t—"

"Definitely not." A shiver runs up my spine. "Sorry. Just... camping is a hard pass for me. But thank you for asking."

"I'm afraid you're out of alternatives, Miss Benton. For this week, anyway. Maybe you can reschedule your interviews and do the article at a later date."

"That's not an option." If I don't deliver on this assignment, I'll be lucky if my boss lets me slink back to the *Trending* page. I've got one shot at this, and it's now. Meaning, it's time to pull up my big-girl panties. Stop being a neurotic mess, if only for the next few days.

Carefully, I get my legs under me. Then, even more carefully, I turn to face him. He's built like a man, but with green scaly skin, yellow eyes with slit-like pupils, and that mouth...

He's just a man. Not really a snake.

I hold my breath to suppress a squeak when his tongue darts out. Is it an involuntary thing, or is he purposely tormenting me? If it's the latter, I deserve it.

It's only a few days, and I shouldn't have to see much of him. I can handle this. Unless that's not an option anymore. "Would you be willing to let me stay here? I understand if you aren't, after all the unintentional, but still awful, things I said."

"The room is yours." His attention shifts to the computer. After a few clicks, he places a tablet and stylus on the customer side of the desk, along with a keycard. "If you would just sign the disclaimer, Miss Benton, I'll finish checking you in so you can get settled."

Is it my imagination, or did he kind of hiss all those words with an *S* sound? Of course, it's me. No news flash on that. It's always me.

LEROY

I haven't seen or heard from Cora since sending her off to unit number two. Unless she snuck out via a rear window, she's still in her room. Even if she had climbed out a window, I would have seen her get into her car and drive away. The motel's layout provides a full view of all six units from the front office.

And I've been watching. Because I'm a considerate businessman and she's a valued guest in Screaming Woods. That's the lie I've been telling myself for three hours.

The truth is, I want to see her again. Which is pointless, and frankly, a bit on the masochistic side. I've never had trouble attracting women—not as a young human man and not in my twenty-one years as a snake man. Once the dust settled on our monster-filled town, single women of all shapes, sizes, and species realized there are benefits to my new physiology. If I want female companionship, particularly of the physical variety, I can have it. Easily.

Maybe that's the reason I want Cora's. She finds me so repugnant, she would rather have stayed in a roach motel than be forced to see me again. She's a lovely, soft, curvy challenge.

After turning things over to my night employee, I step into my office and close the door, then use the desk phone to call Cora's room.

"Hello?" she answers on the second ring.

The front of my pants becomes instantly tighter at the sound of her voice. It's been too long since I was with a woman, that's all. "Good evening, Miss Benton, this is Leroy. I hope I'm not disturbing you. I wanted to check and make sure you're okay. If you're feeling any nausea or other abnormal symptoms, I can call a physician."

"That's so thoughtful, thank you. Aside from the goose egg and a sore elbow, I'm okay. I'm sure I'll be fine."

"Good to hear. If that changes, or you need anything, please call the front desk, regardless of the time. My night clerk will be there until eight in the morning and I've already informed him of your situation. He's at your disposal. His name is Fred, and he's a blob monster."

"A...*blob monster?*"

Based on the incredulous inflection in her question, I'd guess she's wearing a wide-eyed, open-mouthed expression. I bet it's adorable. "Yes. Are you afraid of blobs, Miss Benton?" I ask in a tone I hope she interprets as teasing.

A soft, feminine groan fills my ear. "I don't even know what a *blob* is. I'm so unprepared for this assignment. I had to sign a form saying I'm not afraid of monsters, and I thought I wasn't, but it never occurred to me that the term *monster* could mean practically anything. What if I *am* afraid of blobs? What if it turns out I'm afraid of everyone in town?"

"I'm sure that won't be the case. You were startled by me because of a preexisting snake fear, not because I'm a monster. Why don't you come into the lobby and meet Fred? I'll tell him you're on the way, and I'll stand down the hallway near my private office. I'll be close enough to help if needed, but out of your view."

"I don't deserve your concern and help. Why are you being so nice to me?"

I lean back in my chair, massaging my temples with my free hand. I'm only doing this because she's the first challenging woman to come my way in years and I could use the distraction, not because I care about her. Besides, the article she's writing will be a boost for business. Mine, and everyone else's in town. If it's inevitable for the world to become aware of our monster population, I'd rather it be at the hands of someone down to earth and genuine. Cora certainly seems to fit that description.

"There are a lot of good people in Screaming

Woods who deserve to have their stories told. I'd hate to be the reason you don't hear them."

"Okay," she says softly. "I'll come over and meet Fred."

"I'll let him know."

"You'll be there? Just in case?"

Damn, her voice does things to me. "I'll be there, Miss Benton. Right down the hall."

"Thank you. For everything. I've been staring at my suitcase since I came to my room, trying to decide if I should call my editor and tell him to reassign the story."

"You won't need to make that call." I'll make sure of that, no matter how many strings I have to pull or favors I have to ask.

"I wish I had as much confidence as you do." She laughs lightly, and I swear to God, I feel the sound all the way to my core. "I'm just going to splash some cold water on my face, then I'll be right over."

"No rush, I'll wait for you." In the hallway beside the front lobby. That's all those words mean, no matter how much bigger they feel when I say them.

CORA

After all my ridiculousness, his kindness doesn't make sense. I think he believes I didn't mean to be rude. Even so, most people would have told me to fuck off, or at least washed their hands of me. Leroy continues to do the opposite.

The least I can do in return is try to get a handle on my fear. After freshening up a pinch, I unpack my notebook and pen. If I'm going to meet a blob monster, I might as well be prepared to take notes for my article.

It's just past seven o'clock when I leave my room. The September evening is an idyllic temperature, and the twilight sky is painted in swaths of blue and gold. The Sunnyside Motel sits on a quiet street near the edge of town. A strip of manicured lawn runs along the rear side of the building, and beyond that lies a wooded area. I don't know if any monsters live among the thick trees, but birds certainly do. The air is alive with their happy songs.

I don't hear many birds where I live. My apartment is on the fifteenth floor and overlooks a concrete jungle. The lack of nature was part of the appeal when I signed the lease. I had my fill of wilderness growing up, thank you very much.

The lights are on inside the motel's main office, making it easy to get a look at the monster behind the front desk as I approach. Despite Leroy's green scales, yellow eyes, and black forked tongue, he's still humanoid. He has two legs, two arms, two hands. He wears normal clothes. The same can't be said for Fred.

There's no sign of Leroy when I open the door and step inside. I glance toward the hallway where he promised to be. The area is darkened, but the tingly warmth spreading through me makes me believe that he's there, watching over me. My very own guardian snake. Oh, the irony.

I focus my attention where it should be—on the large, translucent pink monster behind the desk. He has two big, exaggeratedly round eyes and there's an indent a few inches below that might be a mouth. Other than that, he's just... a blob.

"Hi, I'm Cora Benton, the journalist from *B:Here* magazine, doing a story on Screaming Woods and its residents." I extend my arm, embarrassment flooding my cheeks when I realize what I've done. "Oh! I'm so sorry. Habit. Geez!"

"No problem whatsoever," he says as his gelatinous body forms a stumpy arm with three fingers, which he presses against my outstretched hand.

I stop breathing when his cool, smooth substance connects with my skin. At least I didn't pass out or make an inappropriate, insulting comment. *Yet.* The night is still young.

"It's nice to meet you, Cora."

"Nice to meet you, too." Eyes wide, I watch the semi-firm pink jelly retreat, to be absorbed into his essentially shapeless form. Holy shit, I just shook hands a blob monster.

On that note, I open my book and click the button on my pen. "Would you be willing to answer some questions for the article? The tone of the piece will be positive, and you can remain anonymous, if you want."

"You can call me Fred for your story. Better leave it at my first name, though. I have some family members out there who'd probably prefer the world doesn't know they're related to a freak of nature."

"By 'out there,' do you mean outside of Screaming Woods?"

He doesn't have a distinct head or neck, but the motion of his *blobbiness* makes it clear he's nodding. "Has anyone told you about the night we became monsters?"

"Not directly, not yet. The mayor's office provided a statement of events, along with setting up interviews with several residents who changed at the community Halloween party almost twenty-one years ago."

"Ah. I'm sure the documentation about the night we changed is factually correct. Might be lacking personal perspective, though."

"I'd love to hear yours."

Movement in the hallway catches my attention. I glance over again, this time seeing a glimpse of Leroy's back as he turns and walks away. Likely, assuming he's not needed, since I didn't faint or insult his employee. The man probably wants to go home for the day, but rather than come through the lobby and leave, he's waiting where I can't see him. Continuing to be considerate, even though my fearfulness is a direct insult to what he is.

"Fred," I say, turning my head toward him. "May I record our conversation? I'm the only person who will hear it, and I'll delete the recording after I've transcribed my notes."

"Sure." He moves backward and sits—or his version of sitting, anyway—on a stool behind the desk.

My palms are already sweaty, and watching his pink jelly body semi-swallow the dark wooden stool unnerves me to the point of fumbling my phone as if I'm juggling. "I promise I'm much more professional and collected when working behind a computer than I am in person."

"You're doing fine," Fred says with a laugh that's surprisingly human, just like his voice. "I guess you didn't know monsters are real until you got this assignment?"

"Pretty obvious, isn't it?" I smile while setting the phone to record, then place it on the counter.

"Don't beat yourself up about having perfectly natural reactions to us monsters. We've been there. You should've seen the mass pandemonium when half the town morphed all at once. It's been a couple decades, but we were human once upon a time. We know it's a lot to digest."

"Thank you. You and Leroy are both so understanding."

"Well, everything rolls off of me," Fred says, winking one of his big, cartoon-like eyes.

I laugh because it's clearly the reaction he was going for, plus it's funny. I doubt I'd have such a good sense of humor if I suddenly turned into a blob monster.

"And Leroy's a good guy. One of the best," Fred says. "The Sunnyside Motel is a nice place to stay, but I bet the mayor set you up here because of Leroy, not our 4.8 overall star rating on TripAdvisor."

My first instinct is to ask more questions about Leroy. Once my initial fear wore off, I could see he's more man than snake. Logically, I know he's not really a snake at all. Tonight isn't the time for my questions about Leroy. I'll come back another night for that. This is Fred's time in the spotlight.

"Tell me about the night you became something other than human."

"It's okay to say monster. When it became clear there was no way to reverse the changes, most of us learned to embrace them, along with the word monster. If anyone hasn't, well... they won't be on your list of interviewees, so you don't need to worry about them."

"Noted, thank you."

His wide, gummy form shifts side to side, as if he's trying to get comfortable on the stool that's about one-quarter the width of his body.

I have so many questions, most of which are probably far too personal, so I bite my tongue and wait for whatever he decides to share.

"I was seventeen when I went to the town's annual Halloween party with a bunch of buddies. We spent most of the night talking too loud, trying to stand out in the crowd and get the attention of girls from school. Typical teenager stuff. It was going pretty well, too. A cute redhead was laughing at my bad jokes and she smiled when I put my arm around her. I remember thinking 'tonight's the night' as we grabbed a couple of drinks from the refreshment table, then headed for somewhere private to make out. Turned out it *was* the night for something big to happen, just not the thing I had in mind."

Nothing about Fred's tone suggests he's looking for pity or sympathy, but my heart tightens for him, anyway. "Can you tell me about the actual change? Where you were, how it felt—unless you'd prefer to keep those details private."

"I don't mind talking about it. As you can see, I'm a fairly transparent guy." His form shakes with amusement at his own joke. "Not the most transparent monster in town, but I'm sure the mayor scheduled you an interview with Roan, our invisible man. He's a pillar of the community. His coffee shop, Lucky Beans, was one of the first businesses to adapt and cater to all the monster needs and preferences."

"Yes, Roan Byrne is one of my interviewees. I'm excited to meet him, but I'm surprised you weren't on the list."

He does another of what I assume is a shrug. "The mayor's office probably forgot about me. Most people do."

"How is that possible? Are there a lot of monsters like you in town?"

"Nope. I'm the only one."

"Then I don't see how anyone could forget you, Fred. I know I won't."

"That's nice of you to say." His body ripples as he does what I think is a semi-bow.

"I apologize if I'm staring. I'm so intrigued by your...substance. What is it?"

"Nobody knows. Dr. Karloff tried taking a sample to analyze, but needles don't penetrate the surface. I can't be damaged and I don't get sick. Whatever I'm made of, it's completely self-sustaining, so I don't need to eat or drink."

"Wow, that's incredible. Is it possible for you to ingest food or liquid?" This time, I manage to rein in my tendency to blurt out whatever pops into my head, and don't mention his lack of a real mouth. Though I do wonder how it all works, because it really shouldn't.

"Nope, I literally can't swallow anything. Part of that whole, nothing can penetrate the surface thing."

"How do you get around? Is that question too personal?"

"Go ahead and ask whatever you think people will want to know—and that your magazine is willing to print," he says with a laugh. "I can shift my mass in minor, general ways, like I did to shake your hand. So I do that at the bottom of my mass when I moving from point A to point B, or to answer the phone, use the keyboard, open a door, etcetera. But I can only hold those transformations for short periods of time. I can't shape myself into a full person. I'm a basic blob. Not the most exciting or active monster around, so I mostly keep to myself."

Okay, *now* my heart is twisting for him. I'm sure my feelings are written all over my face. This poor man. Does he think nobody would want his company? Have people in town made him feel that way?

"As for the where and how," he continues, either oblivious to my expression or simply lost in his memories, "I was kissing that cute little redhead when the transformation started. It felt like the worst indigestion in the world, and I had to leave her in the front seat of my dad's truck—where we'd been steaming up the windows pretty good—to bolt for the woods nearby. Thought I was going to puke or shit my guts out, maybe both. Then I watched my skin start to change and my clothes tearing apart as I bloated up and my legs disappeared. I thought I was tripping, that somebody had drugged my drink."

"I can't begin to imagine how terrifying that was," I say, hugging myself around the middle. Not a very professional or impartial stance, but oh well. In-person interviews about people becoming monsters aren't exactly part of my average workday.

"There I was, alone in the woods, panicking and

unable to do anything because of the changes happening to my body. Then the screaming started. From my truck, from the party beyond the parking lot…" He exhales, his oversized eyes doing a slow blink. "Things got kind of chaotic after that. Most of the people who didn't turn into monsters left town pretty quick. Some stayed for family. Some tried to stay, but just couldn't do it."

"You mentioned your dad. Were any members of your family affected?"

"No. Fortunately for my parents, they'd skipped the town party that night."

There's a lump in my throat, blocking the question I have no right to ask, except that I do. That's why I'm here—to ask questions. "Are they still in Screaming Woods?"

"No. Unfortunately for me, they also skipped town. Couldn't handle living among monsters, or having a blob for a son."

"Oh, Fred, I'm so sorry." How am I supposed to write a positive, fluffy article about this town after hearing his story? Because I'm sure there'll be others like it.

"I appreciate it, but I'm okay. I don't get out or do much, but I've got a few good friends. I'll leave my number on the desk here. If you feel like a game of chess or Mario Kart while you're in town, give me a call."

"Two of my favorites. I may take you up on that," I say, picking up my phone and ending the recording.

"Thank you for the offer and for the interview. If you leave your email address for me, I'll send you a copy of the article. And if you don't, I'll make sure to send it to the motel, too."

"Will do, Cora." He forms the stumpy arm again, this time using it to make a hat-tipping motion before reabsorbing the temporary appendage into his mass. "Have a good evening, and just call over here if you need anything."

"Thank you." I have so many more questions to ask him. Maybe they'd seem less intrusive during a game. Or maybe it's just that I'd feel like less of a prying intruder under those circumstances. "Goodnight, Fred," I say, giving him a little wave as I leave.

Outside, the peaceful silence wraps around me as I walk the short distance to my ground-floor room. Emotional exhaustion from all the steps I've taken out of my comfort zone slams into me as I turn the key. There's an oversized tub in the beautifully renovated bathroom and it's calling my name. Still, I can't help looking back at the motel office's plate-glass window instead of heading into my cozy room.

There are two monsters in that office. Two men, involuntarily transformed to creatures, now forced to remain in Screaming Woods for the rest of their lives because of humans like Fred's parents. Humans like me.

From here out, I'll do better. No matter what kind of monsters I meet, I'll treat them like the *people* they are. As for the damage I did today... maybe I can mend that, too. Now that I know what to expect when I walk into the motel office, I can control my reactions. It's not Leroy's fault he's a man-sized embodiment of my biggest fear. If he could change back to a regular human, I'm sure he would.

I can change, though. I can be a better person than the one who had the gall to ask Leroy to turn away. I'm not just kicking that version of me off the job, she's fired from my life. I knew this assignment was a turning point, but I assumed it was career related. Now I'm wondering if I'm not here for a bigger pivot...

Chapter Three

LEROY

The motel has six rental units and no vacancies. That's how it's been for years, despite the secluded nature of Screaming Woods. Though some guests only stay short term, others settle in for longer stretches. I prefer it that way, even though the income is less because I reduce the rates. The long-term guests feel more like friends. Like family.

Because of that, I often dress casually for work. There's no need to wear a suit to answer the phone, work on the computer, or exchange a few pleasantries with the handful of people I'll see during the day. Even when new arrivals are due to check in, dress slacks and a crisp shirt are adequate. Yesterday, knowing my incoming guest had been handpicked by the mayor, I wore a suit. I may as well have been naked, because the only thing Cora saw was my skin. And she hopes to never see it again.

Yet, here I am, once again wearing a suit. The odds she'll set foot in the office while I'm here are slim. But if she does, maybe she'll keep her eyes open long enough to see past my scales.

Her feelings about me shouldn't matter. She's nothing more than a client. In a few days, she'll be gone.

Yet, there's more to my attraction than the challenge she presents. More to it than simply finding her beautiful, or realizing that I've reached the limit of my self-imposed celibacy streak.

Despite her reaction when we met, I believe she's a good person. Compassionate. Considerate. Both traits were obvious and sincere during her conversation with Fred last night.

I heard every word from my position in the darkened hallway. Even after I retreated to my private office, I lingered in its doorway, hungry for more of her soft voice.

I shouldn't care what she thinks of me, but I do. I want her to see me the way she saw Fred—as more than a monster. Watching their interaction should have been a relief. Instead, my stomach coiled with inappropriate, unjustified jealousy. The urge to insert myself into their conversation, to force her to look at me—to *see* me—was so intense, I had to get out of earshot. My suite is tucked away in the rear corner of the building, and after locking myself in, I stripped to my skin as a deterrent to leaving the room.

Cora fainted at the sight of my face. I can't imagine her reaction to the rest of my snake anatomy.

Even after a long soak in the tub, sleeping was impossible. I tossed and turned for hours, unable to push her image and the sound of her laughter from my mind. Stroking myself off while envisioning a woman who finds me repulsive shouldn't even be possible, but it was. It absolutely fucking was. I haven't come that hard by my hand since the early years of being a monster. Back then, it was because of being young, overloaded with testosterone, and fascinated with my new anatomy below the belt.

Cora was responsible for last night's shake-me-to-the-core release. Pointless as it is, I can't deny my attraction. I want to strip her bare—of her clothes and her misgivings—and taste every inch of her softness, then sink inside and make her body sing a song just for me. It doesn't make sense, wanting her this way, this much. Illogical things happen. The monsters of Screaming Woods are proof of that.

The motel's main lobby has large panels of glass on two sides, and even though it's unlikely any of my guests would be looking out their windows and into mine, I'm not taking the risk. Some guys can do a quick adjustment when they get an inopportune hard-on. My anatomy requires more finesse. I'm in my private office rearranging myself when the bell out front chimes with someone's entrance. Once everything is repositioned, I step into the hallway. And immediately need another adjustment.

Cora stands at the front desk, chin tipped upward and eyes straight ahead, hands in a clenched ball on the countertop. Not the posture of a woman who wants to be there. Of course she doesn't. Knowing she's about to face me, she's probably struggling to keep her shit together.

Her stature should be enough to deflate my desire. If anything, I get harder with each step toward her. Good thing she's not interested in looking closely at me, because I doubt my recent repositioning is hiding the hardness pressing against my zipper.

"Good morning, Miss Benton," I say, taking refuge behind the high desk. "How was your first night—was everything to your satisfaction?"

Pink floods her cheeks and a small squeak sounds in her throat. "Yes, um, yes. The room feels so homey. And the tub is amazing. I've never been in one that big. It was very enjoyable."

An image of Cora flashes in my mind. Naked and relaxed in the bath, her creamy skin shiny with moisture, the swell of her full breasts breaking through the water, her hard nipples beckoning from just below the surface...

My tongue darts out from my mouth, an involuntary reaction I regret the moment her eyes go wide. "My apologies. I'll try to control the snakier aspects of my physiology in your presence." It's a legitimate

126

offer, but right now, I savor the scent captured by tongue. Thanks to my snake-like senses, I can practically taste her—and she's delicious.

"No, please don't apologize or modify anything for my sake. I'm the visitor here. I'm the one who needs to change, not you."

"I admire your viewpoint, Miss Benton, but I don't want you to be uncomfortable around me, so—"

"Then call me Cora," she cuts in. "Please," she adds, the softness in her voice making me unbearably hard.

My use of her formal name has been intentional. A method of maintaining a professional distance, since that's the limit of our connection.

"I'd really like it if you'd call me Cora. Please, Leroy?" If she were another woman, the flutter of her dark eyelashes might be considered flirting.

Even with a large volume of my blood currently in residence between my legs, I'm not foolish enough to think she has any interest in me beyond necessity. "Cora it is," I say. I like the way her name feels on my tongue. Too much. But that's not her fault. "I'm glad you enjoyed the oversized tub. I had all the rooms remodeled to be monster-friendly when I bought the motel. Although I'm the same height and build as before my change, some of the town's residents increased in size considerably."

"Like Fred."

"And others," I say, redirecting the conversation as unreasonable jealousy flares hot inside me.

"Screaming Woods is home to a lot of large monsters. You might have interviews with some of them."

"I don't know. Except for a note beside Roan Byrne's name that he's invisible, my list of contacts only has names, not... species designations." Her face is bright pink now. "But on my way into town, I did see a really large, um..."

"Monster, Cora. It's okay to say monster. It's what we are."

She huffs in what sounds like internal frustration. "It feels wrong, but fine. The first *monster* I saw was a very large man with dark fur, red eyes, and a huge set of antlers."

"Were you scared?"

"No, I wasn't. But I did gawk at him, of course, because I have no self-control, as you're well aware." She finishes with a light laugh that makes her self-deprecating comment sweet and endearing. "He caught me staring and waved."

"Sounds like Van Bristol. He's a wendigo."

"A wendigo. Another creature—I mean *monster*—term I'm not familiar with." She sighs.

"What monsters *are* you familiar with?"

"Vampire, werewolf, ogre, orc, gargoyle," she says, ticking them off on her fingers. "Zombie, yeti, fairy, invisible man... oh, and phoenix." Her proud nod is adorable.

"We have all of those in Screaming Woods. Plus a lot more."

"Let me check to see if Van Bristol is on my list," she says, dipping into her bag for her phone.

As much as I wish I still had her attention, it's good to see her becoming more comfortable with me.

"He's not on my list. That's too bad. He seemed friendly."

"I think you'll find most of the locals to be friendly. See if any of these names are on your list: Reece Spencer, he's a cyclops and dean of the nearby monster college. Diego Santos is a dragon and a jeweler. There's a satyr named Jace—" *Shit.* I definitely don't want Cora to meet Jace. Not because she'd be afraid of him. The opposite, if the rumors about what he's packing are true. "Vanessa Silke is a cecaelia. Nice lady, very interesting to talk with."

"And yet *another* monster I've never heard of," she says, looking up at me without a hint of fear or reservation in her beautiful aquamarine eyes. "What's a cecaelia?"

"Primarily human from the waist up, with tentacles on the lower half."

"Tentacles?"

"Like an octopus. Are you afraid of octopuses?" I ask lightheartedly. That's my intention, anyway, but it falls flat when she doesn't smile or laugh, only shakes her head.

"No. Only snakes."

Only snakes. The two simple words are like a verbal slap. And I needed it. *I'm* the one getting too comfortable here.

"Right. Well, I'm the only snake man of my type in town, but there is a naga. Also, twins who both became gorgons after sharing a bottle of punch at our ill-fated Halloween party. Their *hair* is...lively. Based on your reaction to me, I think you should avoid all of them, if possible. If you want me to look at your list of interviewees, I'd be happy to."

"I don't know what a naga or a gorgon is, either."

"A naga is mostly man up top and snake on the bottom. Gorgons have serpents for hair, like Medusa."

"I..." She swallows hard. The earlier blush is completely gone from her face. Even with her current drained pallor, she's still the prettiest woman I've laid eyes on in as long as I can remember. "God, I'm so out of my depth here. I don't know why my editor chose me for this assignment."

"Your editor didn't choose you. The mayor did."

Cora's head twitches as she jerks backward. "She did? How do you know that? And why me?"

"She mentioned it when she reserved your room. I assumed she chose you based on your body of work."

The laugh that bursts from Cora's mouth isn't the same as the one I heard last night, during her exchange with Fred, or the sweet sound from moments earlier. This version is harsher. Humorless. "My body of work definitely didn't qualify me for this assignment. For the last three years, literally every column I've written has been about clothing, makeup, dating, or sex."

And...I'm fully hard again. Speechless and a little

confused about the mayor's choice to pen an important article, but also really fucking hard. Cora writes about sex? I know what I'll be reading tonight. Every last damn column.

Sighing, she slides her phone across the desk. "Here. Could you check the list and see if I should politely cancel any interviews?"

"Of course." Without picking up her phone, I scroll the names, places, and times of her interviews for the duration of her visit. The mayor has set up a lot of stuff, all of it which should go smoothly. "If you don't have any other monster or creature fears, you'll be fine. No one on this list is in any way reptilian. I'm the only snake you'll have to see."

"Okay, good." Another of the little throat noises squeaks out of her, this one slipping through her parted lips. "That didn't sound the way I intended it to. I meant, it's good that I'm seeing you."

"Is it?"

"Yes, it is." She reaches over, I assume to retrieve her phone, but I'm wrong. She extends her arm fully while making dircct, unwavering eye contact. "I'd like to start over."

"Are you sure you want me to touch you?" I ask, glancing at her waiting hand. "I'm pretty thick-skinned, but if you scream when we shake hands…"

This time when she laughs, it's the kind that buzzes through me like a live wire. "I'm not going to scream. Or faint."

"I like the confidence, but this is a quick one-eighty from yesterday."

"Not totally quick. I thought about this all last night."

"You thought about shaking my hand? All night?"

"Yes," she says softly, her eyelashes fluttering like hummingbird wings. "I thought about you a lot, actually."

Was she thinking about me during her long, 'very enjoyable' bath? The odds of that are unlikely. My body couldn't care less about the odds, it's primed and humming as my mind revisits the mental image of Cora in the tub. Except, in this version, she's touching herself and moaning my name.

Shaking my head to dislodge the erotic fantasy, I raise my hand and take hers.

Her eyes open wide the instant our skin touches, but she doesn't scream. Doesn't pull away or look lightheaded. Her pupils enlarge and a soft exhale leaves her parted lips, then she smiles and curls her fingers around mine. "Hi, I'm Cora Benton, a writer with *B:Here* magazine and a socially awkward intro-vert who should probably get out more, but really doesn't want to."

Smiling is a risk because she might see my fangs, but it's impossible to keep a straight face in the pres-ence of this much cuteness. "How do you write columns about dating and sex if you don't get out much?"

"Honestly?" She pulls her full bottom lip between

her teeth, then leans toward me and whispers, "From romance books."

"Not personal experience or clinical research?"

"Zero," she says, another pretty pink flush sweeping across her face. "Not *literally* zero, ever. I do look things up after I read about them. And I'm not a total nun, I have... you know. Just not to the extent or, um, *variety* my columns might lead readers to believe."

I like this information a hell of a lot more than I have any right to. This woman is never going to be mine in the way I'm craving, but there's some satisfaction in knowing she doesn't belong to anyone else, either.

When the phone rings, *saved by the bell* has never been truer. I need a reason to break contact because common sense isn't doing the job. Just because she's being friendly doesn't mean she sees me as anything more than a one-hundred-and-eighty-pound version of her greatest fear.

"Go ahead," she says, motioning at the insistently ringing interrupter. "Oh, but do you have a piece of paper first?"

Nodding as I answer the call, I place a notepad and pen in front of her. The motel is always booked, and searching the schedule for a workable vacancy takes longer than expected.

It's hard to focus on the call while Cora walks away. She doesn't seem like the type who consciously tries to be sexy, and that's one of the reasons she is. Her soft curves certainly don't hurt. The way the material of her short skirt pulls taut across her round ass is the stuff of dreams, and her shapely bare legs in tall black boots will haunt my waking mind until I see her next. Which, according to the note she scrawled and left for me, will be tonight.

> If you're not busy, I'd like to continue our new start later. If you're interested.

If I'm interested. Thank God for the tall desk I've been standing behind, or she'd have seen just how interested I am. And *that* would definitely send her away screaming.

Chapter Four

LEROY

Less than an hour has passed when Cora's rental car turns into the motel parking lot. The premature return isn't something to worry about—she could have gone out for something to eat before her first interview this morning. It's the way she slams the car door that piques my concern. It's her hunched shoulders and red, tear-streaked face when she glances toward the office before disappearing inside her room.

If she wanted my help or support, she would've come to the office. Or she'd call the front desk. Neither thing happened, and why would they? We're not friends. We're barely acquaintances. She's a client. A woman who had to psyche herself up just to look at me.

Apparently, none of those things matter because the next thing I know, I'm standing at her door, knocking as if I have a right to. I step back at the sound of the lock turning, then the door swings inward, and any trace of common sense remaining vanishes.

I cross the threshold before she has the chance to invite me in or send me away. "Why are you upset?" I ask, carefully closing the door behind me. Shit, maybe she went to the Sweet Things bakeshop and came face-to-face with one of the gorgons. Checking the list of names wasn't enough; I should've told her places to avoid in town.

She shakes her head, making the tips of her light-brown hair brush her shoulders. "I don't belong here."

"Few humans do." *And I want her to be one of them.* "What happened to make you feel this way? Did you accidentally run into one of the monsters I suggested avoiding? I should've warned you to steer clear of the Sweet Things bakery. I apologize if that's the cause of your unhappiness."

"That's not it." A gulping sob hitches in her throat. "Fred said you're a good guy, and he's obviously right. I appreciate your patience and support, but today proved I'm completely wrong for this assignment and this town. Once I get control of my emotions, I'm going to call the mayor and let her know that I'm leaving. Hopefully she'll choose someone else from *B:Here* to take my place, but if she doesn't, and it costs me my job, then it does."

She's visibly shaking, and the urge to take her in my arms almost gets the best of me. Being hugged by a snake would send her running from Screaming Woods faster than I can swallow my breakfast whole. Once she's gone, I'll never see her again. I'm not ready for that.

"What happened?" I ask again, taking a step backward in hopes it'll reduce the tension in her posture. "Maybe I can help."

"Why would you?"

"Because I'm a good guy, like Fred said. And I don't want you to leave."

"Someone else will come to write the article," she says, hanging her head and hugging her arms around her middle.

"I don't give a shit about the article, Cora."

Her gaze snaps up to meet mine, her eyes opening wide when I step closer. Close enough to touch her, which I do, because apparently, I'm not *that* good a guy. Her long-sleeve shirt prevents skin-to-skin contact when I curve my hands around her arms, but my body reacts to the sensation, regardless. Fortunately, my suit jacket is buttoned, hiding the evidence of my wildly intense attraction.

"Tell me what happened so I can fix the problem and convince you to stay."

"You can't fix *me*."

The words hit me the way they should—as a

reminder that my very physiology is her problem, meaning I'll never be her solution. I drop my hands to my sides. "Let's focus on what upset you this morning. Maybe I can assist with that."

Emotion swirls in her blue-green eyes. "I had an appointment to interview the invisible man who owns Lucky Beans, the coffee shop downtown."

"Roan. I've known him since we were human. We played football together in high school. He's a private man, but thoughtful and decent. I can't imagine he'd be anything other than friendly— unless he thought you had designs on his woman. I'm kidding about the last part. Aside from a one-off moment when Roan mistakenly believed I was interested in the love of his life, we've always gotten along."

"The woman who works with him in the coffee shop? The one with the spiky quills?"

"Ah, you met Melinda." Something must've been going on for Mel to have her quills up. They lie flat most of the time, making them generally unnoticeable. "No, Roan and Melinda are just friends. Roan's lovely lady is a human from out of town, though she fits in as if she's been in Screaming Woods forever."

Somehow, Cora's expression sinks lower. "I've never felt that way about any place. I wish I did."

That's my wish too, and I want the place to be here. I push the pointless pining aside to focus on the present. "I don't go into Lucky Beans often, but I know it's a nice little coffee shop, casual and comfortable, very welcoming to all comers, monster and human alike. What happened there that upset you so much?"

"I was waiting in line to ask for Roan. The place was fairly busy, so there was the usual noise of people talking and equipment running. But then, suddenly, there was a high-pitched shriek that rattled the windows, and a pink-haired fairy flew up to the ceiling. A dragon-like man with wings burst through the door, followed by a dark-haired man who looked human but seemed to be something more, and a woman brandishing a baseball bat. The human guy who'd been sitting with the fairy was flipping out. The invisible man's disembodied apron and gloves were floating around, and it was just so much, I-I freaked out. I turned around and left without saying a word."

"I'll make some calls and find out what the commotion was about, but I assure you, that kind of thing isn't the norm for Lucky Beans or any establishment in Screaming Woods."

"Then maybe it's all me. The universe is sending me signs that I'm not supposed to be here. I can barely handle being around ordinary people, and I'm obviously not equipped to for face-to-face contact with monster people." Looking toward the ceiling, she throws her hands up in a gesture of frustration. "You win, okay? I don't know why you brought me here, but I give up, I'm going home."

My stomach tightens when she grabs her suitcase, drops it open on the bed, then begins loading it with her clothes. "You were great with Fred. No issues at all.

I know because I watched and listened to the whole interaction."

"I thought you went into your office after the first couple of minutes. I saw you walk away."

"I backed off when I could see that you didn't need assistance, but I didn't leave." Because I couldn't. Just like I can't now.

"Well... that conversation with Fred was an isolated incidence of me not losing my shit. It doesn't count for much after the way I reacted today, or worse, the way I totally freaked out when I met you."

"You're not freaking out around me now," I say, moving closer. It's a ballsy move, but I catch her wrist before she can reach for the next item of clothing. When she doesn't balk or pull away, I push her sleeve up, making this a skin-to-skin touch. "How are you now, Cora?" Saying her name while holding her, even this way, feels intimate. "Are you scared of me?"

"No," she whispers. "Not at all."

"What about now?" I let my tongue dart out, watching her eyes go wide at the sight of it. "Does my tongue frighten or repulse you?" I press it to the roof of my mouth, barely suppressing a groan when I taste her scent.

Her pulse hammers in her throat as she shakes her head. "I'm getting used to it, it's—it's just a tongue now. The more I see of you, the less I see a snake, and... the more I see a man."

"Good," I say, releasing her before I do something she'll be less accepting of, such as sweep my forked tongue into her mouth. "You'll get used to the other monsters in town, too. You just need to see them doing everyday things in a situation where there's no pressure on you."

"Are you suggesting I stalk them? Because you've seen enough of me to know that's not going to be a success. I'm not built for subtlety or stealth. Besides, I've already missed one interview, and the next one is later this afternoon—if I can even pull myself together for it. I don't have time to do advance creeping of the monsters."

"What if I could help with that? Completely aboveboard, no creepiness whatsoever? Would you trust me and try it before throwing in the towel?"

"I want to, but I think I'm wound too tightly for anything to work."

Oh, if only she'd let me help her *really* unwind. I could make her feel as if every bone in her body is pillow soft. She'd be so relaxed, she wouldn't know if a band of sasquatches walked by. Since that's never going to be an option, I'll take a different route.

"How about this—I'll get someone to watch the office for a while and we'll go out for a ride to clear your head. After that, if you decide you're willing to give my zero-creepiness, totally normal idea a try this evening, I'll call Lucky Beans and whoever you're supposed to interview this afternoon to reschedule your appointments."

"You'd do all that to ensure the article gets written?"

"Fuck the article," I say, throwing professionalism to the wind. "I'd do all that and more to get you to stay."

She pulls her bottom lip between her teeth, releasing it slowly, teasing me to rock harness without even trying. "Okay," she says softly. "I'll go for a ride with you to see if it helps clear my head."

Victory rings my heart like a bell, even though logically, I know she said yes to the opportunity, not to me. "I'll head back to the office and arrange for someone to swing by for coverage, then get changed for the ride. Do you have jeans and a short sweater or jacket?"

"Um, yes." She glances down at her skirt. "I can't just wear what I have on to go for a ride?"

"Not for this ride." Smiling is risky because I don't want my fangs to scare her further away. Since she doesn't seem to mind my tongue, I let it dart out. "Have you ever been on the back of a motorcycle, Cora?"

CORA

Apparently, everything about this trip to Screaming Woods will be outside my comfort zone, even an activity that's supposed to relax me.

Telling Leroy I've never been on a motorcycle didn't dissuade him. He just added, "make sure your ankles are protected" to his instructions, then left me to get changed.

I'm familiar with motorbike safety. I grew up on a rural property with two brothers who rode dirt bikes. Even on those small bikes, the pipes got hot enough to burn through lightweight fabric—and skin. I know this from seeing it happen. There's a reason I've never been on a motorcycle, just like there's a reason I'm afraid of snakes. And my brothers are responsible for both fears.

Backing out of Leroy's genuine attempt to help would be a shitty thing to do, so I'm dressed to tackle another fear—as much as my suitcase wardrobe can accommodate. Leather chaps and a protective, padded jacket would be great. Skintight jeans and my knee-high leather dress boots from earlier will have to do. My hip-length blazer is far from ideal, but it's the closest thing I have to a jacket. The upside? If this is how I die, I'll look good doing it. The clothes I purchased based on the last *Trending* column I wrote are every bit as snappy and form-flattering as I promised readers they would be.

I'm pacing fast enough to wear a groove in the floor when a knock startles the bejesus out of me. My heart leaps into my throat and the room begins to spin. I can't do it. As much as I want to conquer my crazy and walk away from this trip with a bold, shiny new path in front of me, realistic me knows all I'm equipped to do is the "walk away" part. I'll thank Leroy for his kindness and efforts, then finish packing and get the hell out of town before I waste more of his time.

Decision made, I take a deep breath and open the door. "Hi-oly shit." My jaw drops and stays there. I don't know what I was expecting, but this is not it. I've seen Leroy in a suit, and there's no denying the man knows his way around business wear.

But this? Leroy in chunky motorcycle boots, jeans that are the perfect amount of broken in, and a black leather jacket over a white V-neck shirt... The snake man is sexy. Yes, I said it.

"You look beautiful."

"Thank you," I say, using the response as a way of collecting my bottom lip from the floor. My body is already reacting to his hotness, but the heat cranks up several notches as his yellow eyes do a full perusal and his tongue slips from his mouth more than once. I googled that physiological twitch last night. Snakes use their tongues to smell, and then, in a way, to taste. Does it work the same way for Leroy? Is he *tasting me* when his tongue slithers out?

"Is that the only jacket you have?" He tilts his head when I nod. "It's a warm day, but it's always cooler when you're out on a bike. If you get too chilly while we're out, yell at me and I'll head back to the motel. Okay?"

"Got it." Now I have an excuse for cutting this

adventure short without hurting his feelings or admitting I'm scared of yet *another* thing.

"You're welcome to leave your purse and keys behind so you don't have to carry them. We can use the master room key from the main office when we get back."

"You don't have saddlebags on your bike?"

"No," he says, his mouth curving with what appears to be a hint of a smile, as much as that's possible with his features. "When I go out on the bike, it's not to do shopping."

"Then I'll leave my things here." I empty my pockets and toss my purse on the bed, then gather what remains of my wits and shrug. "Ready."

"Perfect." He opens the door, holding it for me to walk ahead.

Doing so requires passing in front of him. It's not the first time I've been this close to him, but now it feels different. The others were accidental or out of necessity. This seems...personal.

"Is that it?" My abrupt stop on the sidewalk that runs along the front of the rooms causes Leroy to bump into me.

His hands land on my hips and remain there as his "Yes" tickles the shell of my ear.

"It's exactly the same green as your skin." God, I'm so lame. Just call me the queen of ridiculous observations.

"Custom paint job." He moves away from me to

retrieve and hand me a helmet. "It's a Ducati Monster."

"It's a green Monster."

He shrugs. "Cheesy, I know, but I couldn't resist."

"I love it," I say as the first smile I've had since the coffee shop chaos pushes my troubles away. For now, anyway. It remains to be seen how long I'll be able to hold the panic at bay before using the excuse Leroy provided to end the ride. Until then, I'm enjoying seeing another side of him. Less pulled together and serious than suit-wearing, motel-managing Leroy.

"Do you need help with your helmet?" he asks after settling his on his head.

Because, duh, I'm still staring at him while holding the hard, white shell he gave me. I pull the helmet on, wiggling and shifting until it's as comfortable as becoming a bobblehead can feel.

The narrow slits of his yellow eyes focus on my fingers where I'm fiddling—and failing—with the chin straps. "May I?"

"Yes, please."

"I'll try not to touch you, but my fingers may graze your chin while I tightening the strap."

"I don't mind." The words slip from my mouth as easily as breathing. As honestly, too. In the course of one day, I've gone from losing my shit at the sight of him to not freaking out at all, to thinking he's sexy. There may be hope for me yet. It's more than that, though. I'm not just *unafraid* of the snake anymore. I'm interested in the man.

A shiver ripples through me when the back of his hand brushes my skin. "Sorry about that," he says, stepping back.

"Don't be. I'm not."

"Nor should you be." His snake features aren't as expressive as a human face, but if a voice can frown, his just did.

"Wait," I say, grabbing his arm before he mounts the bike. "I think—I think you misunderstood me. When I said I'm not sorry, I meant I'm not sorry you touched me. I didn't mind. At all. Okay?"

He nods, just once, then swings his leg over the bike and motions to me with his left hand.

"Um, where am I supposed to sit?" The green Monster is nothing like the big touring bikes I've seen in the movies.

"Here," he says, patting a small area behind him. "It's called a pillion seat. Not the most comfortable place you'll ever sit, but I promise you won't even notice once the wind therapy kicks in."

"Wind therapy?"

"You'll see what I mean." He points to a short arm sticking out from the bike, above the pipes. "Put your foot on the peg, then grab my waist and bring your other leg over, the way I did. There's a peg for your right foot on the other side."

Grab his waist. Grab the sexy snake man—who I was terrified of just yesterday afternoon—by his waist. Maybe none of this is real and I'm having the wildest dream of my entire life.

"I'm holding the bike steady, Cora. All you need to do is make sure your foot is secure, then use me for leverage. Nothing will go wrong."

"That's not a challenge you want to throw out to the universe when I'm part of the equation."

His shoulders rise and fall with his laughter. "The universe and I are good. We made peace a long time ago. Trust us both and get on the bike."

"You're a brave man," I say, settling my boot where he indicated. I grab fistfuls of his leather jacket, then haul myself into place on the tiny patch of leather that's allegedly my seat. "Now what?"

"Flip your visor down, wrap your arms around me, and hold on." Even with his head turned to the side, his black helmet blocks his face from view.

I can hear him, though, and this time, there's definitely a smile in his voice. And I like it. I like it a lot.

Chapter Five

CORA

Best. Thing. Ever.

I don't know how long we've been out. There were a few minutes of fear initially, but once I got used to the motion of turns and sensation of being *in* the wind, time ceased to exist.

Leroy had told me to wrap my arms around him and hold on, and that's exactly what I did. At first, it was out of fear I'd fall off the motorcycle. My reason for *remaining* wrapped around him had nothing to do with fear.

I liked the solid warmth of him while I was pressed tight to his broad back. Once, he took one hand off the handlebars and pressed it over mine, where I had them clasped in front of him. I thought it was affection until he drew my hands upward. I hadn't realized they were resting *below* his waist. I thought that hard bulge beneath my hands was the rolled edge of his jacket. Um, no. Apparently, I was holding his cock. Embarrassing? Oh my God, yes. But also...wow. That was one heck of a bulge.

Maybe riding the green Monster gives the green monster a hard-on. I wouldn't judge him for it. The combination of the Ducati's engine rumbling beneath me and having my legs spread with my extremely under-used lady parts pressed tight to Leroy's butt had my body buzzing.

Did I subconsciously fondle his crotch because I was horny? Strong maybe. Will I have to take the edge off my newly awakened desire when we get back to the motel? Most definitely. I've never been much of a self-pleasure enthusiast, but I've also never felt such an intense need for release.

The motel comes into view sooner than I'm ready for the ride to be over. I loosen my hold as he pulls into the lot, shifting my hands to the sides of his jacket when he parks near the office door.

He kills the engine, flips up his visor and says, "Passenger gets off first."

"As soon as I'm in my room," I whisper in the privacy of my helmet.

"Need any help with that?" he asks once we're both back on solid ground.

Oh my God, he heard me. Wide-eyed, I blink at him, my mouth hanging open.

"The strap." He motions to my fingers, where they're motionless beneath my chin. "Want some help?"

"Oh!" Shit, my face is as hot as a raging inferno. He must think I'm insane. Or an idiot. Probably both. "I, um... I think I've got it." A little more fumbling and the strap slips free.

"I've got this," he says, carefully lifting the helmet from my head. "Let me grab the master key so you can get to your room."

"Thanks. And thank you for the wind therapy. I really loved it. I haven't enjoyed an activity that much in years." More heat rushes to my cheeks when he chuckles. "I told you I don't get out much."

"No judgment here. Just a large desire to be part of more activities you'll enjoy."

Is he...flirting? Could that have been a sexual innuendo? No, he's just friendly. The same friendly guy he was before my clit woke up after its years-long slumber and decided to flood my brain with thoughts of sex. Sex with him.

"Now that you're feeling more relaxed, can I convince you to give my other idea a try?"

The one with the monsters, plural. I can already feel the tension seeping back in, just at the thought of another encounter like at the coffee shop. After everything he's done for me, I should at least hear him out. "What did you have in mind?"

"A bunch of us meet at the park on Tuesday evenings for a friendly game of pickup football."

"You want me to play football with monsters?"

"No, not play," he says, not even trying to hide his amusement. Nor should he—laughing looks good on him. "I want you to be the prettiest spectator we've ever had the pleasure of tackling each other in front of."

"Oh." Now *that* was flirting, right? God, I'm so out of practice with men, I can't even tell.

"We're just a group of buddies throwing the ball—and sometimes each other—around. Same as you'd find in any town or city in the country, except with fur, wings, tales, and scales. Come and watch. Seeing us doing normal, everyday things might help you feel more comfortable during your interviews."

If he's right, I could be back on track for the magazine piece tomorrow, rather than tucking *my* figurative tail between my legs and running away from this opportunity. "Okay, I'll go. Just tell me when, where, and how I need to dress."

"Whatever you wear will be perfect, Cora. I'll knock on your door at quarter to seven."

"You think I won't show up unless you take me."

"That's not it at all. I want to be the envy of every unattached monster in town when you get out of my car," he says, then opens the motel office door. "I'll be right out with your room key."

That was *definitely* flirting, right? I hope.

CORA

I'm not a sporty girl. I probably know less about sports than I do about monsters. But after watching Leroy run up and down the field in a pair of black athletic shorts and a light-gray T-shirt that's now sweat-soaked and sticking to his lean, muscled upper body, I'm a new fan of football. Don't ask me to explain the rules of the game because I'm still clueless about the how. I only know *why* I suddenly like it, and he's currently shaking hands and buddy-slapping the other monsters on the field.

"Good game."

"Nice play."

"Thought you were going to send me to the hospital with that tackle in the end zone."

Everyone Leroy talks to on the way off the field gets a different comment. My snake man is one heck of a people person.

My snake man. There's a thought I never in my life expected to have. Still, it lingers, warming me from the inside out as I enjoy the last few seconds of prime ogling time remaining.

"Well," he says when he reaches the small set of wooden bleachers where I'm sitting. "How do you feel about us monsters now? A bit more at ease?"

Honestly, if he handed me a pop quiz requiring me to list the different monsters who'd shared the field, I'd be lucky to get the minimum passing grade. Not because of the variety is too much to remember. They just didn't register in my brain. I was too busy watching Leroy.

"I don't feel scared at all," I say, omitting the fact that I'm referring entirely to him.

"Perfect. That means you'll be unpacking that suitcase when you get back to your room."

I nod because it's less of a fib than using words. He doesn't need to know I unpacked after the motorcycle ride. Okay, technically, I unpacked after the *post*-motorcycle-ride activity, which took more time than I thought it would. Apparently, I had a lot of pent-up stuff to get out of my system. The way my body is humming right now, it would seem there's still more.

"Ready to go?" he asks, collecting his small duffel bag from the bench beside me.

I give another nod as I hop to the ground. "I really enjoyed watching you play."

"And I enjoyed watching you watch."

"You barely stood still for two seconds. I'm surprised you had time to notice."

He meets my gaze as our feet crunch the parking lot gravel in synchronized steps. "I noticed. I haven't been able to stop noticing since you walked into the motel yesterday."

My heart is pounding in my chest by the time we reach his car, where he opens and holds the passenger door for me. "You saw the note I left you last night, right?"

"I did."

"It's probably too late for dinner now, but maybe we could do that tomorrow night, since I'm staying in town to write the article?"

"I'd love to take you out," he says, his tongue flicking out.

Heat rushes through me at the sight of it. His tongue didn't make an appearance during the football game, I'm sure of it. "Does your tongue work the same way a regular snake's tongue does? Can you smell with it?"

"Yes," he says, holding my gaze.

"Is it involuntary, or do you control it?"

"Both." His tongue darts out again, lingering longer before retreating into his mouth. "And in both cases, the more I enjoy the scent, the more of it I want to capture."

Desire beelines straight between my legs. "How fine-tuned is it? When you capture my scent, for example. Is it always the same?"

"Each person's scent is unique to them, so in that regard, it's always the same. But other factors can affect and vary your scent."

"Like, what someone has eaten?" I ask, holding my breath for his answer.

"Yes. I can always tell when a person has eaten onions, garlic, cloves, or cinnamon."

"Is that a good thing or a bad thing?"

"They're not scents I enjoy."

Note to self—avoid onions, garlic, cloves, and cinnamon while I'm in town, especially tomorrow at dinner. "What are some scents you *do* enjoy?"

"Excitement is one of my favorites."

Oh, shit. Does he mean *excitement*, excitement? "And here I was thinking more along the lines of strawberry or lemon."

My attempt at humorous redirection earns me a chuckle. "Snakes are carnivores."

"But you're not an actual snake. You have arms and legs, and—" I bite my tongue before the names of some other body parts I've been ogling find their way past my lips. His shorts may be dark and loose-fitting, but I haven't forgotten how great his butt looked in the jeans earlier, or the size of his bulge beneath the zipper. Snakes don't have *those* body parts.

Mercifully, he lets my embarrassment slide. "Some might think I was unfortunate to become part snake the night we became monsters. It's not how I would've chosen to live my life, that's true. But I have the best of both species within me. I embrace my snake qualities just as much as my human ones."

"If someone came along tomorrow with a cure, would you take it?"

"Are you asking for your story, or for personal reasons?"

"I wasn't thinking about the assignment when I asked." I haven't thought about the article for a single moment since I opened my door to find a sexy-as-sin snake on the other side.

There's a long pause before he nods. "I'm sure you'll get a variety of answers to this question, but mine is no. I've been a snake my entire adult life, longer than I was human. This is who I am."

Nodding, I slide into the passenger seat. But Leroy doesn't close the door. Instead, he leans in, his athletic, green-scaled body filling the frame as he meets my eyes. "Your interviews tomorrow are with Fynn, the yeti who lives up the mountain, then Ryett, a wyvern whose cabin is in the woods. Neither place is the easiest to get to, and GPS isn't always reliable around Screaming Woods. How would you feel if I went along as your chauffer?"

"That would be wonderful, but you already took most of today off work to hold my hand."

"I'll take every day off if it means I get to hold your hand, Cora."

"I'd like that." I'd like it even better if he meant it literally. Maybe tomorrow. "Is your gnome friend available to fill in for you again?"

"No, Jerry's busy tomorrow, but I've already made arrangements for someone else to sit behind the desk."

"First, your gnome friend, now someone else. In addition to getting the motel covered, you also rescheduled both the interviews I missed and neither person who I stood up today seemed to mind. You sure don't have any trouble getting people to do things."

"Reverse snake charm," he says, his tongue darting out as he chuckles.

Butterflies take flight in my belly and chest as I smile at him. "I know it's working on me."

LEROY

I knocked on Cora's door this morning wearing jeans and a long-sleeve T-shirt that hugs the biceps she kept looking at, before and after last night's football game. I was athletic before becoming a monster, and since I was fortunate to retain that aspect of my prior physique, I put in the effort to maintain it.

Our lifespan as transformed monsters is an unknown. Even the old scientist responsible for the change can't hazard a guess. Dr. Karloff claims he tried to create a "good mood enhancer" for the community Halloween party twenty-plus years ago, only to realize far too late that he'd used an incorrect ingredient. Some people believe it was intentional. Either way, it's done, and like I told Cora, I've made peace with what I am. Whether I have one more day or one hundred more years, I plan to make the most of my time.

Today, I was happy my time involved Cora. She didn't *need* my help. She could've found both monsters' cabins from the map the mayor provided. I wasn't worried about her reaction to Fynn or Ryett. Neither are snake-like and they're both decent guys, though not the most social. That's why it surprised me when her interview with Ryett ran longer than expected. After getting all of her monster questions out of the way, they started talking about the chainsaw sculptures he sells online. Turns out Cora is a fan of handcrafted items. Information I'm tucking away for future use.

Their extended conversation meant skipping lunch —fine by me, since I'm dreading having to explain why I'm *not* eating. Dinner tonight is plenty soon for that inevitably unpleasant revelation.

From Ryett's cabin, Cora and I headed straight to her third appointment, the one originally scheduled for yesterday afternoon. This should be an easy interview for Cora. There's nothing threatening about Jenni Harper. Aside from some feathers, the siren looks like a human woman. Jenni's siren voice doesn't affect monsters the way it does humans, but she doesn't need it. Her beauty and uninhibitedness are a song in themselves. When Jenni wants male attention, she gets it, song or no song. Her monster story should make for interesting content.

My seat is reclined and my legs are kicked up, sticking out of the driver's front window when Cora exits Jenni's house alongside the bright-eyed siren. I right myself in a hurry, then get out of the car to go around and open the passenger-side door for Cora. I've heard chivalry is dead in the world beyond Screaming Woods. As long as I'm breathing, I will always put ladies first. One lady in particular, if things go my way.

"Ladies," I say, nodding when the pair reaches me. "Always nice to see you, Jenni. Keeping busy with the music students?"

"Not so busy that I'd say no to a ride on the green monster." Her siren song may not affect me, but that doesn't mean I can't hear it in her voice. It's a sound I knew intimately a year-or-so back.

Cora's gaze bounces from me to Jenni. "You've been on Leroy's motorcycle?"

"No, honey. His *other* green monster," Jenni says without giving Cora the courtesy of looking at her. "Or would you say monsters? Which is correct, Leroy? What are we calling the one-eyed snakes these days?"

Shit. "Jenni's just teasing," I say, motioning Cora to get in the car.

"Oh, lover," Jenni croons. "You know I *never* tease."

Double shit. "We'd better get going, so Cora isn't late for her next appointment."

"Yes," Cora says, smiling at Jenni and following my lead. "Thank you for taking the time to speak with me. I'll send you a copy of the article before it publishes."

"Can't wait." The words slot perfectly with Cora's comment, but when Jenni swats at my butt as I pass, it's obvious she meant them for me.

"I guess you and Jenni are close," Cora says after I've pulled away from the curb. Her attention remains forward, with not so much as a peripheral peek in my direction.

"Not anymore. Not in over a year."

"Well, I think she'd like to get back together with you." In her lap, Cora's fingers knit together until her hands are one tight little ball. Is she jealous? She sure looks and sounds it.

I'd be happy as fuck if I wasn't worried that Jenni's big mouth had ruined things. "Jenni and I were never together as a couple." I glance over, but Cora doesn't turn her head or shift her eyes from the windshield. "And even if she is interested in reconnecting, I'm not."

Silence fills the car as I make the short return trip to the motel. There are no more interviews today. I lied to get the hell out of there before Jenni said something that'd make things worse, which she could have, if she'd volunteered further information about our former hookups.

As I close in on the motel, I reach over and cover Cora's fisted hands with one of mine. "I'm sorry for putting you in that uncomfortable situation."

Now she looks over at me. "You don't owe me an apology or an explanation, but..."

"But?" I ask, working her clenched fingers loose so I can weave my fingers between hers.

"But it would have been nice to know I was interviewing one of your ex-whatever she-wases. I wish I'd known before I started talking."

"Would it have changed the questions you asked?"

"No, but it would've changed the things I *said*." Bright pink flares on her cheeks. "I don't know why I volunteered so much information."

"What information?"

"Just...things. About you. About me. Mostly about you." A little grumble that's probably frustration but sounds adorably kitten-like passes through her lips. "One minute I'm asking her questions from my list, and the next minute I'm—" She shakes her head and pulls her hands from beneath mine.

"The next minute, you're what?" I ask as I turn in to the motel lot. Parked in my regular spot beside the office, I shut off the engine, then gently catch her beneath the chin and turn her face toward me. "Did Jenni sing for you?" I can picture it as if I were there— Jenni offering a sample of her voice so Cora can describe it for the article. "She's a siren, Cora. That's how they get humans to do their bidding."

"And you think she did that so I'd talk about you?"

"It's possible. I probably pinged on her radar when I called to reschedule your interview. Then I took you to football last night, and I've never taken a woman there before. Monsters gossip just as much as humans do, so she may already have heard about that through the grapevine. Today I'm driving you around... If she thinks there's something happening with us, I could see her trying to get in the way of that."

"Because she wants you back."

I shake my head. "She didn't want to be with me

before, not in a real relationship sense. But she also didn't want me to end things."

"You ended it because you wanted a serious relationship with her?"

"Not with her, necessarily. I just wanted a relationship. I was tired of women coming to me for a good time. I was ready for someone to want me for all the other times, too."

"Did you ever find that someone?" Cora asks softly.

"There hasn't been anyone since." Fuck it, I'm going for it. I sweep my thumb across her bottom lip and lean closer. "Not until you."

"Are you going to kiss me?" she whispers, her pupils dilating when my tongue darts out. "Is it possible for you to kiss me?"

"It'll be different from what you're used to because my mouth isn't shaped like yours."

"I'm not used to anything. I write columns about dating and sex, but I haven't had a boyfriend or a date since I got the job."

That's three years. She told me she's been writing columns for three years. I don't know how the male human population has so completely missed the boat, but I'm not going to do the same.

"Do you—" She pulls her bottom lip between her teeth, worrying it until it's moist and ruby red.

"Ask me anything, Cora, and I'll give you an honest answer. I may be a snake, but I don't hide. I'll tell you anything you want to know."

"Do you bite?"

"Only if you want me to, sweetheart," I say, letting my mouth widen to the closest thing I have to a smile.

"Is that a thing? Have you been with women who wanted you to bite them?"

Telling her about past encounters is the last thing I want to talk about, but I told her I'd answer anything. "Yes. Some people enjoy the bite. If it's not for you, I won't do it and I'll never miss it."

"But you like it. The biting. You like doing it."

"I like giving pleasure. What that includes is different for each person."

"How do you know what someone wants? How would *I* know if I want something when I've never had it?"

"Discovery and experimentation are part of the pleasure," I say, circling her wrist with my fingers and bringing it to my mouth so I can press a kiss to her pulse point.

"Your lips are drier than I expected. And firm. Not like mine."

"A lot things about me are different from human anatomy."

Her eyebrows rise and her mouth forms a generous O that would look so pretty around my cock. "You're talking about your..." Her gaze falls to my lap. "Is that what Jenni meant by *your other green monster?* That it's different?"

If there's a chance this is going where I hope it is, best I lay the cards on the table now. "Aside from fearing snakes, do you know anything about them?"

"Not much. I know that some are dangerous and some aren't, and it's not always obvious which is which. I grew up in a rural area and snakes were common in the yard and the woods beyond. My older brothers used catch corn snakes and garter snakes and torment me with them. Pranks with harmless snakes, I know, but I was scared of them, anyway. Then, one day, when I was nine, I was out in the field, and my brothers starting yelling at me to get away from the snake. I thought they were making fun of me, and I decided to put an end to it by showing them I wasn't afraid to touch the stupid snake. It turned out to be a rattler, and it didn't appreciate my show of bravery. Worst moment of my life."

And there it is. The trauma that made her faint when she met me. An experience that has stayed with her for twenty fucking years isn't just gone in a couple of days, no matter how much I want it to be. I shouldn't even have joked about biting her. Thoughtless idiot. It's a wonder she's still in the damn car with me.

Her eyebrows draw together when I withdraw my hands and ease back, giving her space. "I told you all that because I want you to know, to understand my crazy better."

"You're not crazy, Cora."

"That's a matter of opinion and a lot of people who know me would disagree, but it's good you feel that way about me."

"I feel a lot of ways about you. Ways I have no

business feeling after what you've experienced. After knowing you for only a few days."

"Then I must have no business feeling the way I do, either," she says, shifting in her seat to face me. "But I'm not going to apologize for the things I'm feeling or pretend they're not there." She sighs when I don't respond. "Everything about this is new for me. And it's scary, but not because I'm afraid of you. That's over. I don't see a snake when I look at you. I see a man."

"But I *am* a snake." I open my mouth wide enough to put my fangs on display. They sit alongside a short row of human teeth that remained after the transformation. My fangs are small compared to a real snake's, but they're long and sharp enough to pierce skin. "If I kiss you, you'll feel my fangs, even without a bite."

"It might take getting used to, but if you're patient with me, I will."

"You shouldn't have to 'get used to' kissing someone, Cora."

"Isn't that for me to decide?"

Ignoring her question, I move to the next item I know she'll find repugnant. "When we go out for dinner, I won't order from the menu because I don't eat the same food humans eat."

"Okay, then we won't go out. We'll stay in and cook whatever you like."

"I don't cook *anything*. My meals are always raw."

"Like sushi?" she asks in a small voice.

I shake my head. This is where my time with her

ends. As I knew it would, even though I tried to fool myself into believing we were at the start of something great. "I'm a carnivore who swallows my food whole, as snakes do, because that's what I am. I eat mice, frogs, slugs, worms, bugs...and other prey creatures. Sometimes they're dead, and sometimes they're not. But they're never cooked, and I haven't chewed my food in over twenty years."

"That's..."

I can see the wheels turning in her beautiful head, and I know where those wheels will take her—as far away from me as possible. I knew she'd leave Screaming Woods and never return. Expecting anything else—hell, hoping for another outcome— was pointless from the beginning. Since I've driven her this far, I might as well take her the rest of the way.

"I only drink water, and not a lot of it. I have one of the oversized tubs in my unit, too, and I have to soak in it nightly. That's how I get most of my hydration, through my skin. As for Jenni's comments about my green monster—or monsters—just like my snake relatives, I have two."

"Two...what?"

"Two cocks. Snakes have two penises. That's one of the physiological traits I inherited when I became a monster. Except snake penises are held within their body until needed, and mine are not. They're on the outside, the same position and size as a human penis, but now I have two."

"And they both, um... function?"

"Completely." In fact, they function so well, they're both hard right now, simply because I know Cora's thinking about them. Single-minded damn body doesn't give a shit that I'm not her type, because she's mine. I've never wanted anyone the way I want her.

Motion inside the office snags in my peripheral, and I turn to meet my brother's gaze through the glass. He points at the phone in his hand, then at me, giving me the thumbs-up when I nod.

I turn back to Cora while hitching a thumb toward the office. "My brother's flagging me that there's a call I need to take."

"That's your brother?" Her eyes open wide as she stares into the office. "He's human."

"Jimmy was too young to go to the Halloween party. He was only ten at the time."

Lines form between her eyebrows and her lips move as she mentally does the math. "He's thirty-one?" she asks, and I nod. "I'm twenty-nine. I never thought to ask how old you are."

"Forty."

"Well, you don't look a day over snaketeen," she says, smiling.

Cute. So fucking adorable, I have to consciously hold myself back from taking the kiss we almost had.

"Your brother is handsome," she says, a soft blush coloring her cheeks as her eyelashes flutter while she holds my gaze. "He's a bit pale for my liking, but handsome."

"Would you like me to introduce you?"

"No, but go and take the call. I've eaten up enough of your time." She unbuckles her seatbelt and opens her door, pausing with one foot in the car and one foot out. "Thank you, Leroy. Your patience, kindness, and honesty have changed, well...everything."

"You're welcome," I say, waiting until she closes the door behind her to add, "Miss Benton."

I'm alone again, a solitary snake. Despite the constant flow of guests, friends, family, and available lovers, I'm alone. Of all the snake characteristics I possess, this is the only one I wish I could change. Watching Cora cross the parking lot and enter her room without a single look back, I know my future is a narrow path I'll be taking alone.

CORA

He was going to kiss me. Would have kissed me if I'd been able to control the flow of mood-killing comments that left my mouth. Even when I want to be flirtatious or seductive, my awkwardness messes things up.

Groaning aloud, I roll onto my stomach and press my face against a pillow. Instead of asking if he was going to kiss me, I should have told him to. Better yet, I should have made the move and kissed him. We could be in his room right now, kissing and touching, or more…

Longing and awareness tugs between my legs, and I slide my hand under my prone body, pressing two fingers against my clit. I've masturbated in this motel room more times than I have in my apartment, where I've lived for three years. Even the few times that I did, it was forced and lackluster. Like a duty I had to fulfill to have any semblance of legitimacy as the author of *how-to* sex columns. I was a fraud. A skittish, complacent automaton skimming the surface of living.

Living and being alive are two different things. I know that now. I came to life when I met Leroy. Even in that initial moment of fear, I was more alive than I'd been in… I don't know how long, and that sensation of rawness and vulnerability was terrifying.

I was nine years old all over again, wanting to hide from the monsters. To run away and block out everything that's not guaranteed safe. Consciously or not, that's how I've lived my entire life. That's not how I want to live the rest of it.

I'd rather be scared than numb. I'd rather risk feeling pain than miss the chance of feeling everything else.

Even after everything he told me, there's a lot I don't know about Leroy. And the things I just learned are…significant. The differences between us should probably scare me, but when I imagine how his teeth, tongue, and skin would feel against mine, there's no spark of fear, only the tingling desire to feel all of it. All of him.

I could have told him that in the car. When he was trying to scare me away with his snakish facts and I didn't have the tiniest urge to run away... I could have told him right then that it wouldn't work. That none of those things matter because I'm falling in love with *him*.

I'm still not going to tell him. Tonight, I'm going to *show* him.

Chapter Six

CORA

I smile and wave as I enter the motel office. "Hi, Fred."

"Nice to see you, Cora. How's the article shaping up?"

"Really well," I say, stopping at the desk. "Leroy took me to watch monsters play football, and today I had three very interesting interviews. Tomorrow I'm meeting with the invisible man who owns Lucky Beans, and the fairy who operates the library. Then I have an appointment with the mayor that I'm excited about."

"Sounds like you're getting nice and comfortable here."

"I am. Actually, I'm going to talk to Leroy about the possibility of a long-term rental."

Fred's already-large eyes open wider and the little divot below them becomes an upward-curving line. "I'm sure he'll be happy to accommodate that request."

God, I hope so. I nod while hitching the shopping bag higher onto my shoulder. "We had dinner plans tonight. Is it okay if I go back?"

"Of course." Fred's pink jelly pushes outward to form a stumpy arm aimed in the direction of the hallway leading to Leroy's private office, and farther along, to his suite. "Have a good evening."

"Thanks, Fred. Don't work too hard."

"No chance of that," he says, moving in a way that makes his gelatinous form jiggle.

I'm still smiling from Fred's joke when I knock on Leroy's door for the first time, hopefully of many. My smile becomes open-mouthed gaping when the door swings inward.

Leroy stands just inside the room, one hand braced on the door. He's bare-chested and barefoot, his green skin glowing with the sheen of fresh moisture. A pair of light-gray sweatpants sit low on his trim hips, and it's entirely obvious he's not wearing anything underneath. To say it's a lot to take in is an understatement.

"Sorry, I thought the knock must be Fred. I wasn't expecting it to be you, or I would've put on better clothes," he says, taking a step back.

"I don't think there's a woman out there who

would complain about what you're wearing. Or is 'gray sweatpants season' not trending here?"

"There's no season for gray sweatpants in Screaming Woods. We wear them year-round."

I bite the inside of my cheek, but it doesn't prevent my giggle from escaping. For a man who seems to be aware of pretty much everything, he's totally oblivious. "There's no actual season for gray sweatpants, Leroy. It's a saying. A term women use while appreciating the way a man looks in gray sweatpants, because of the, um—" I make a swirling motion toward the significant package visible in the front of his pants. "Outline of things."

I understood the memes, but never fully appreciated them. So what if you could see the outline of a dick? I get it now. I really get it.

As much as I'd like to explore my newfound appreciation with this holy grail of gray sweatpants, that's not why I'm here—and it's not the kind of attention Leroy wants or deserves.

"I brought dinner," I say, patting the bag I'm carrying. "It doesn't make sense for us to go out if I'm the only one who'll be able to eat, so I called around, then picked up things we'll both like. May I come in?"

"After what I told you, you want to have dinner with me." The words leave his mouth slowly, as if he's trying to make sense of a riddle.

I nod. "Yes, I was surprised by the information. A little shocked, even, and I think that's understandable since I'm new to the monster world. But I didn't freak out, and I never said I wanted to cancel our plans. Do you?"

"I think it's best if we do."

The urge to retreat to a safe place where rejection isn't an option flickers inside me, but I stomp it out by standing my ground and holding his gaze. "That doesn't answer my question. I asked if you want to cancel our plans. Simple yes or no."

"There's nothing simple about what I want with you." He steps aside, his arm outstretched in invitation. "I'd very much enjoy your company while you eat dinner."

"While *we* eat," I say after he's closed the door behind me. "I know I've given you every reason to doubt what I can handle. Now I'm asking you to give me a chance to handle more. Please let me try, Leroy. Because I want to try everything with you." I set the bag down and pull out a package of flash-frozen mice the owner of the pet-supply store told me Leroy purchases regularly. "I want to understand how you eat."

"I don't eat in front of people."

"I'm not 'people.' Or at least, I don't want you to think of me that way. I don't want to be *people*, I want to be your person." I close the distance he put between us, the package in one hand as I place the other flat on his bare chest. "Eat with me. Then, after, kiss me, and... whatever comes after."

"*Cora*." His tongue darts out as I slide my hand

over his skin, exploring the contours of his muscles beneath his scaly, textured skin.

"I'm not scared of you."

"Then the tables have turned," he says, as I trail my fingers over his face. "Because I'm scared of the endless ways in which you'll break me when you leave."

"I'm not leaving." We can talk about my plans for the column and staying in town later. Right now, I want to *show* him I'm exactly where I want to be. I catch his hand and lace our fingers together, sparks racing up my arm at the sensation of his skin against mine. "Let's eat."

He lets me tug him along to the table for two, where he sits stiffly, his yellow gaze following me as I open the cabinets in his small kitchenette.

"You don't have any dishes." I give myself a little tap on the forehead. "Of course, you don't. You swallow your food whole."

"Cora—"

I cut him off with a headshake and a smile. "We'll get some for me. We don't need them tonight, anyway. We both have finger food."

"You want to buy dishes to keep in my kitchen?" he asks as I take the seat across from him and place our respective containers of food on the table.

Heat licks at my cheeks. "Or we can eat at my place, wherever that ends up being. Sorry, I didn't mean to overstep on the first date. Don't worry, there are no tampons in my bag that I'm planning to stash in your bathroom cabinet." I give him a wink. "Not yet."

Even with his limited facial expressions, his confusion is apparent, and I can't help giggling. I unwrap my takeout order and pop one of the sushi rolls into my mouth, chewing and swallowing as he continues to stare. "I'd offer to share, but these have rice and seaweed in addition to the raw fish, and you said you're strictly a carnivore. I made sure there's no garlic, onion, cloves, or cinnamon, though." I make a circling motion at the package in front of him. "Eat something. The sooner we get through this part of the date, the sooner we can get to the kissing."

With obvious trepidation, he opens the bag and removes one of the mice. "They're not cold."

"The clerk in the store suggested bringing them to room temperature, so I stopped in my room and used the microwave. If that's not right, though—"

"It's exactly right, Cora." Eyes on me, he says, "Are you sure about this?"

"It's your turn to trust *me*." Bold words out in the world, I hold my breath as he tips his head back and opens his mouth unbelievably wide. Mesmerized, I watch the rigid, dead mouse disappear into the gap, then follow the lump as it moves down his throat, and ultimately, out of sight.

Mouth closed, he straightens his posture, locking his eyes with mine. "You didn't faint."

"You'll have to do something more exciting than eat to make me faint during dinner."

"I'll keep that in mind for the future." He rises from his chair, moving around the small table and guiding me to my feet. "Thank you. I stopped eating around people a long time ago because of the reactions it receives."

"I told you," I say, sliding my hands up his chest and twining my arms behind his neck. "I'm not *people*."

"No, you're not. You're a special person. My person." He dips his head, pausing only long enough to dart his tongue out before touching his mouth to mine. His skin is firm and warm, and even though our shapes are different, we match up perfectly. The sensation of his fangs pressing against my lips, knowing he could bite me, but won't, sends a flurry of awareness to my core.

My breath hitches when his tongue slips between my lips. He weaves one hand into my hair and cups my head, adjusting the angle of our kiss as his tongue moves against mine, then all around. The forked points tickle the roof of my mouth and I squirm, pressing myself tight to him. The large, hard bulge of his cocks pushes against my abdomen, and the sparks of need between my legs flare into wildfire.

Beneath my palms, his back is smooth yet textured, broad at the shoulders and tapering to a lean waist. My fingertips graze the edge of his sweatpants, and I slide my hands down to cup his butt, pulling him closer.

"Don't stop," I whisper when he breaks the kiss.

"Never. This is only the beginning." His tongue flicks against the column of my neck, then into the hollow at the base of my throat.

I hum as he licks across my collarbone and into the neckline of my scoop-neck top. "You can take it off," I say, meeting his eyes. I haven't been naked with anyone in over three years, but I'm not afraid of what happens next, because it's with him. "I want you to take it all off."

His hands find the hem of my shirt and peel it up, over my head. My bra drops to the floor next, then his tongue is on me, sliding and flicking over my breasts, teasing my nipples until they're hard, sensitive peaks.

My head rolls to the side when he sucks one nipple into his mouth, continuing to flick it with his tongue as he sucks. "I'd tell you never to stop doing that, except I want you to do it other places, too."

"I plan to, sweetheart." He curls his fingers over the edge of my leggings and wiggles them down, past my hips, taking my panties along with them. "I've wanted to taste you since the first day I captured your scent."

"When you told me one of your favorite scents is excitement, did you mean... you know." Heat races through me as he drops to his knees in front of me, lifting my feet one at a time so he can divest me of all remaining clothing.

"I meant the scent of your pussy, Cora," he says, licking a path up the inside of my thigh. "Your arousal." He flicks his tongue between my legs, a groan rattling in his chest. *"You."* Then he's on his feet, lifting me off mine, his warm breath tickling my ear as he strides to the bedroom. "I need you spread open for me. I want you pinned down by my tongue. I want to watch you fly apart when it's inside you."

"Nobody has ever talked dirty to me." I giggle against his neck. "Mind if I use it for a column?"

"Give me until your interviews are wrapped up and I'll make sure you've got a lot of source material."

I keep my arms around his neck as he lays me out on the bed. "What if I want more than a couple of days?"

"How many more do you want?" he asks, holding my gaze.

"As many as I can get. As many as you want to share with me."

"You can have all my days." He dips down and presses a single kiss to my lips. The next kiss is on my neck, then he's working his way down, zigzagging across my breasts before licking a hot path that crosses my bellybutton and ends with his face between my legs. He takes one long, slow lick that parts my folds, then looks up my body and into my eyes. "I'll give you as many days and nights as you let me."

"Looks like I'm going to have a lifetime of source material."

Eyes locked with mine, he licks me again, then again. Flicking, jiggling, nudging me deeper into pleasure. The fork of his tongue cradles my clit, framing it for his fingers.

My hips tip up to meet the perfect rocking pressure of his touch. I moan, my hands slide over his smooth head, desperate for purchase as the first stirrings of climax mount.

"Not yet, baby. I'm not done tasting you. I want your sweet nectar rolling down my tongue when you come on it."

Oh, yes. There will be plenty of source material for my future dirty-talk column.

"Oh God," I gasp as he slides his tongue inside me. Deeper, deeper, it just keeps going. Unfurling, seeking, and—

A strangled cry leaves my lips when he flicks his tongue against some spot deep inside me while massaging my clit with his fingers. My body rocks beneath him, and all I can do is moan and ride the wave of orgasmic euphoria.

I shiver as his tongue retreats. It's thin and narrow, yet the loss leaves me feeling empty, needy to have him inside me again.

"So good," he says, sliding his tongue through my wetness. "My new favorite thing to eat."

My hips have a mind of their own, rising to meet his attention. Tempted as I am to enjoy more of his tongue, I want the rest of him, too. "How does it—I mean they—work? Your, um—*ugh!*" I clap my hands over my face. "Why can't I say it? I write about sex stuff all the time, and... I mean, God, you just made me —you know."

His laughter is muted by his position between my

spread thighs, but the vibration of it is like gasoline on my already-primed fire. He presses his mouth to my center, then crawls up the bed, with my body caged beneath him. "I do know. I was there when you came, and it was delicious." Gently, he peels my fingers away from my face, then looks down at me with his equivalent of a smile. "Cocks. Say it with me—cocks."

"Cocks," I whisper, the heat of mad embarrassment rushing to my cheeks. "Is my face bright red? It must be, I can feel it." I groan. "Why am I this way?"

His body shakes with silent laughter. "Adorable? Beautiful? Determined? Resilient? Generally sexy as fuck?"

"You left out awkward."

"I didn't." He cups my chin in one hand and brushes his thumb over my jaw. "It's part of every other trait I mentioned, and I wouldn't change it, or a single thing about you."

"I wouldn't change anything about you, either," I say, amazed at the truth of my words. "I mean it. With all my heart." I twine my arms behind his neck and pull him closer. "But you're going to have to tell me how it works with two cocks—there, I said it— because I've never even *pretended* to know about that."

Chuckling, he drops a quick kiss on my lips, then presses his forehead to mine. "It works however you want it to." Arms wrapped around me, he takes me along as he rolls onto his back. "There are no rules. No limits. No pressure."

The very large, incredibly hard bulge in his pants

presses against me from beneath. If I rocked on him, even a little, I'd come. But I want him inside me when that happens.

I shimmy downward, my thighs bracketing his knees as I curl my fingers beneath the waistband of his pants. "Can I be a jealous, possessive girlfriend and say that these gray sweatpants are for my eyes only? I know you've been with other women, but—"

In a blink—mine, obviously—he's sitting upright, his hands cupping my face as he takes my mouth is a hard kiss. "There are no other women, Cora. The past doesn't matter, and you're the only one I want in my future. You'll never have a reason to be jealous, and if you want to be possessive of me, that makes me the luckiest monster or man in the world."

"So... you'll save the gray sweatpants just for me?" Teasing is safer than saying the big little words threatening to spring up from my heart.

"Just for you, sweetheart," he says, lying back. "Now, take them off me and get possessive of my cocks."

"Ooh, more dirty talk for my column?"

"More telling you how I feel because I want you to know."

"Even better." So much better, I almost spill *my* guts right now. I wiggle the gray fleece down his hips. The waist elastic catches on his big package, and I bite my bottom lip as my fingers graze the two tips while I free them. A gurgled gasp pushes past my lips once the full length of both cocks come into view. "They're so..."

"Snake-like," he says, when I fail to form further words.

It's the unfamiliar uncertainty in his voice that pulls my attention from the mesmerizing view below his waist, up to his face.

"If your fear of snakes makes this more than you can handle, either now or always, I'll understand."

My gaze returns to his cocks. He's right that they're snake-like. Each one is long and thick, the same green as his brightest scales, and similarly textured. The slightly flared tips do resemble serpents' heads, but when I look at them, snakes are the furthest thing from my mind.

"I'm not afraid *of them*, only that I won't be able to take them." Because they're long. Really long. And thick. Much thicker than any single penis I've encountered in my limited experience. "Can I just... try stuff?"

"Try anything and everything you want," he says, propping onto one arm so he can reach my chin. "Do what feels good for you and I guarantee it'll feel fucking great for me, because I'm doing it with you."

No one has ever made me feel as wanted, cherished, and respected as this man does. I inch backward, tugging his pants completely out of the way. Then I crawl between his legs, wrap one hand around each of his cocks, and draw my hands up the shafts. I pause when a low hiss rises from his mouth. "Is that okay?"

"More than okay. Just having your hands on me feels so fucking good."

"Then let's see how my mouth feels." Leaning forward, I draw the flat of my tongue up the length of one cock. Rows of small scales give him a subtle texture I can't wait to feel inside me. Holding him at the base, I close my lips around the tip and hollow my cheeks as I descend. I don't remember what any other cock tasted like, but Leroy's is warm and vaguely earthy, and I moan around his thickness when his tip hits the back of my throat.

"It feels amazing." He moans as I suck hard on the upstroke. "So fucking amazing."

Fueled by his words and my building buzz of desire, I pick up the pace, bobbing up and down one cock while pumping the other with my fist. I shift my position, changing the angle to get more of him into my mouth. With each downward stroke, I take him deeper, and when my nose bumps his abdomen, I hold him there, savoring the heft of him in my throat.

"Much more of that and you're going to make me come."

I hum, sucking hard until I let him pop from my mouth. "I want you to."

He hisses as I suck him into my mouth. "Just one," he says, stilling my hand on his other cock. "Saving that one to bury in your pussy."

The ghost of what's next tightens the longing tug between my legs. I slot my fingers with his where we're gripping his second cock, then double down on the one in my mouth.

His hips flex upward to meet my urgent, sloppy,

sucking strokes. Then his free hand tangles in my hair, holding me in place as his cock throbs in my mouth. "Cora, *fuck...*"

Thick, hot spurts splash deep in my throat, and I swallow them down until there's nothing left, and he shudders beneath me. His chest rises and falls as if he's just run several lengths of the football field, and when I let his cock slip free of my mouth, his entire body twitches.

"Is it always that—intense?"

His fingers sweep across my face, tucking my hair behind my ears. "We'll find out next time."

"Because the past doesn't matter," I say, remembering his earlier words. "You really meant it."

"Every word."

"In that case..." I slide our joined hands up his other cock until it pops out of our grip. "You'd better bury this inside me, like you said."

"That's not what I said, sweetheart." He takes his hard shaft in hand, his tongue darting from his mouth, capturing my scent. "Tell me exactly where you want me to bury this cock."

Heat blazes in my cheeks and between my legs. "In my pussy," I whisper.

His tongue darts out again as he rolls me onto my back and settles between my parted thighs. "Now say it again for me."

"I want it—"

"Not 'it,' sweetheart. Use the good words. The dirty

words that make your face turn that pretty shade of pink."

"I want your cock—" My breath hitches as he notches the head of his hardness at my entrance, the tip nestled teasingly between my folds.

"Keep going, baby. Your voice makes me so fucking hard, Cora. I hear it in my mind when I'm stroking my cocks at night."

I moan when he slides deeper inside me. "Bury your cock in my pussy," I say, wrapping my legs around his hips. "I want all of it."

"That's my beautiful girl." He fills me fast and fully, hissing a moan when he bottoms out. "Fuck, you feel so good. So perfect."

"*We* feel perfect." With anyone else, this would be too soon. Except there wouldn't be anyone else. He's the one I didn't know I was waiting for. The only one I'll ever want.

He kisses me hard, his mouth meshing with mine as he thrusts inside me, filling me to the hilt. Between us, his other cock is hard again, pressing against my clit and nudging me closer and closer to the edge of release.

Everything tingles, I'm so close. So, so close. My hips arch to meet each deep, lingering thrust, desperate for that little bit more to push me over. "I need—I need—"

"I've got you," he says, shifting position so he's on his haunches with my hips angled up on his muscular legs. His tongue flicks out, teasing my nipples, first one, then the other, back and forth as he grips my hips and fucks me even deeper. The tip of his cock hits that magic spot—the one I've written about but didn't believe was real until his tongue proved otherwise.

Stars explode behind my eyelids as my orgasm slams into me, hard and soft, like the crest of a powerful wave and its soft ebb. Like waves, it keeps going, with every thrust of his cock inside me, every slide of his cock over me, until I'm panting and moaning and pleading. For more. For less. For him.

"Cora." My name leaves his mouth like a reverent prayer, then a shudder racks his body and he throbs inside me. "Cora," he says again, blanketing my body and stroking my hair. "I don't want to scare you away, but there's something I need you to know."

"Whatever it is, I can handle it. And if it's something I'm not prepared for that makes me lose my shit —because I am me, after all—it still won't scare me away, because I know you're right here to help me."

"I'm always going to be here to help you. But I hope this is one time you won't need it." He rolls onto his side, propped on one arm and looking down at me with his hypnotic yellow eyes. "I love you. I think I started falling in love with you the minute you walked into my life and fainted at the sight of me. It didn't make sense, but somehow, I knew my life was about to change."

"A turning point," I say softly.

"The biggest one of my life."

"Second biggest. Becoming a snake was the biggest."

He shakes his head. Strokes my cheek. Leans in and presses his mouth to mine for a long, gentle kiss. "The day I became a monster was about me. The day I met you was about *us*. Meeting the woman I'll love for the rest of my life was the biggest turning point." He loves me. He's in love with me.

"I love you, too," I say, blinking fast to hold back tears but failing as they break free and roll down my cheeks. A half sob, half laugh chokes its way past my lips when he darts his tongue out to capture the rogue drops. "Do snakes like salty things?"

"They don't taste like salt, sweetheart. They taste like happiness. They taste like love."

Exactly as they should, because they're all about him—*my* big turning point. The last man I could ever have expected to love, and the only one I ever will.

Chapter Seven

LEROY

Running The Sunnyside Motel solo has never been a problem. It's a small operation, easily managed with only minimal assistance. Working long days alone is a good choice for a solitary creature like a snake. Today, though...

Today, the minutes feel like hours, and the hours feel like days. Not only because Cora isn't here, but because I'm not the only male anxiously awaiting her return. The only man in the physical sense, yes. But her editor—a growly, impatient man with no phone manners—has called the motel's main line three times since midafternoon.

When he said he couldn't reach her on her mobile,

I tried to myself. I'd resisted until then. The way to a woman's heart is not through her cell phone, no matter how much I think she'd enjoy a string of emojis containing snakes, eggplants, and cats, along with a detailed description of how those symbols represent my plans for tonight.

Her editor was correct. Cora's phone goes straight to voicemail, and the mailbox is full, probably with messages from her editor. Text messages show as *Sent*, but not delivered or read.

Worrying and overreacting aren't part of my nature. Whatever life hands me—positive or negative—I make my peace with it, use it to the best of my ability, and carry on. A survival mechanism, yes. Also, an efficient and sensible way to enjoy life.

My method isn't serving me well at the moment. I know Cora's schedule—the places, the people, the times. She should have returned hours ago. Even if her mysterious meeting with the mayor ran long, there's no way she's still there. The city hall offices are long since closed.

Shit. Day one of our official relationship and I'm ready to go into obsessive boyfriend mode.

I have the phone in my hand to call Fred in early when Cora's rental car pulls into the parking lot. The coil of tension in my stomach eases, then relaxes some more when she steps out of the car looking unharmed and happy.

We spent the better part of last night fucking, and Cora woke me this morning by stroking both my cocks to hardness before climbing on top and fucking each one until I came as hard as if it were my first time. My body forgets all those moments of intense satisfaction when Cora opens the car's rear door and leans inside, putting her sexy ass on display. I want her now. I want her every day for the rest of my life.

My patience is pretty solid most of the time, but waiting another minute to be near her isn't possible. I'm out the door and at her car before she backs her pretty ass up, and when she does, she backs it into me.

"Oh!" she says, then, *"oh..."* when I wrap my arms around her and hold her tight against the bulge of my rock-solid cocks. "Feels like you missed me. I don't know how that's possible after everything we did in the past twenty-four hours, but I'm not mad about it." Her soft giggle is like a rocket to my heart.

"It's possible because I love you." I can't touch her the way I want to while we're in view of so many windows, so I nudge her head to one side and slide my tongue down the column of her neck. "I'm never going to get enough of you. Every chance I get to taste you and fill you, to make you come...I'm going to take it."

"God, I hope so." Her voice is breathy and a flush of pink paints her creamy cheeks. "What time does Fred get here, so we can go to your room?"

My room. That needs to change. "Thirty minutes."

"Perfect," she says, turning in the circle of my arms, then sliding hers around my neck. "Just enough time for me to get things ready."

"The only thing I need is you."

"Well, good. Because I need you, too. And when I'm needy, watch out. I'm like a bad smell—you'll never get rid of me."

I dart my tongue out, smiling when her lips part at the sight of it. "You smell delicious. I know what's on my dinner menu."

"I can be your dessert." She pushes up to her toes and kisses me. "I have a surprise for dinner. Do you have time to help me with a few bags?"

"I always have time for you, with or without baggage."

"Ha-ha, Mr. Funny." She gives me a playful swat before turning to the car to retrieve multiple shopping bags from a variety of stores in town. "I've got these, if you can get the ones in the trunk?"

"Now I know why you were late. The Screaming Woods Chamber of Commerce thanks you for your support." I take the key fob from her hand and use it to open the trunk. "But why was your phone turned off?"

"Because I'm one of those people who can't *not* answer if it rings." The light, relaxed smile fades from her face. "And I'm expecting a call from the magazine that might not be what I want to hear."

"Whatever they have to say, they're determined to say it as soon as possible. Your editor left three messages at the desk this afternoon. He wants you to call him, ASAP."

"Shit," she says, her shoulders sagging for reasons other than the weight of her shopping bags.

"Is it about the article?"

"Yes. Sort of." She hangs back when I head toward her room with the two bags I collected from the trunk. "Um... those are going to your room." Rosy pink tints her cheeks as she bites her bottom lip. "All the bags are—but don't worry, it's just part of the thing I had planned for tonight. None of it has to stay, and I promise you won't open your bathroom cabinet later and find a box of tampons," she ends on a giggle.

So cute. "What if I want to?"

Little lines form between her eyebrows, and her nose scrunches up.

I close the distance between us and look into the sea-colored eyes I could swim in forever—and hope to. "The parking lot isn't the place I planned to have this conversation, but when the time is right, you don't wait. And there's never going to be a better time to tell you I want to start a life together than right now, because I don't want to miss a day we could've shared. I don't want to miss a minute."

"What are you saying?"

"I'm saying I want your box of tampons in the bathroom cabinet. *Our* bathroom cabinet. I want the dishes I hear clinking in these bags on our kitchen shelves. I want a moving truck to pull up tomorrow and unload everything you own into our room."

"I've never lived with anyone," she says softly.

"Neither have I."

"How do you know I won't drive you crazy with my crazy?"

"I won't love you less if you do. I'm only ever going to love you more, Cora."

The shopping bags on her arms drop to the ground. I barely have time to carefully set the break-ables I'm carrying down before she launches herself at me. I catch her as her arms and legs wrap around me, koala style, and she buries her face against my neck.

"You ruined my surprise."

"Your surprise was to inform me you're moving in with me?" A laugh shakes through me when she catches my skin between her teeth like an angry little kitten.

An adorable little huff tickles my neck, then she pulls back so we're face to face. "The moving truck is scheduled to be here next week. Soonest I could get."

I wait for the punchline, but it doesn't come. "You're serious."

Her hair shimmers in the late-day sun as she nods. "About moving to Screaming Woods, yes. Not *here*, here."

It takes every ounce of my patience not to jump in and tell her that *right here* is the only place she should live.

"I pitched an idea to the mayor. Instead of *one* article about all of Screaming Woods, I suggested a recurring column, each focusing on a different monster, business, or event. If Screaming Woods is going to open its doors to the normies, I think it makes sense to really highlight everything that makes this place special. Not just a spit shine—the glossy deluxe treatment. Plus, there are some really wonderful arti-sans and entrepreneurs here who have online busi-nesses. Being highlighted in a national digital magazine could really help."

"That's a great idea."

"The mayor loved it. My editor wasn't as receptive to the pitch."

"Is that why he's been calling all over, trying to reach you—to tell you to finish the assignment and get your ass back to the city?"

"That was his original answer. But I rejected it. I told him he could either give the new column a chance for a year, or I could quit and take it to another publi-cation. The Screaming Woods feature is the mayor's idea, after all. She can hire whoever she wants to publish it. *B:Here* doesn't have rights to anything yet."

"Then why avoid your editor's call? It sounds like you're holding all the cards."

"On paper, sure. But if my editor calls my bluff, I'll have to quit. I may not find a home for the monster column immediately, if ever. It'd be easier to find a job in my field while living in a city, rather than here, in a semi-secret town. Guess I'll know after I talk to him whether I should cancel the moving truck. My shit isn't as together as the shopping spree suggests." Sigh-ing, she disentangles from my body and returns to solid ground. "No big surprise there, I know."

"Everything about you has been the best surprise of my life," I say, catching her hands. "Now that we've found each other, nobody gets to decide our future except us. I want to feel you beside me in bed every night and watch you take a ridiculous amount of time chewing breakfast food every morning. I want to help you when you need it and be your biggest cheerleader when you don't. Call the moving truck and change the delivery address to the manager's unit at The Sunny-side Motel, where the rent is free and the owner's number-one priority is your satisfaction."

"He is very good at his job." Her giggle is like sunshine on the cloudiest day. "But then what?"

"Then call your editor and thank him for the opportunity, because no matter what his decision is, you're going to kick ass with this project. I believe in you, Cora. I love you. Be here with me. Always."

"There's nowhere I'd rather be," she says, a big, round tear sliding down her cheek as she wraps her arms around me. "I love you, too. Take me home."

Epilogue

LEROY

Cora's shriek has me dropping my call and running down the hall to our door. After a year together, I've learned to distinguish between the variety of noises she makes. Usually, the shrieks she makes while inside our suite are pleasure-induced. Like last night, when we—

"Thank God you're here!" She flings herself at me the moment I open the door, wrapping herself around me in a hold that'd give any constrictor a run for the money.

"Is there another spider?" I ask, twisting left and right to survey the nearby area. Spiders are one fear I hope she never overcomes. I love coming to her rescue when she sees one. Plus, they're a spicy treat I don't often have the opportunity to enjoy.

"No snacks. You'll have to wait for dinner," she says, giggling as she shimmies down from my arms. "I got an email!" She squeals again, this time with an adorable little dance that ends with a double-fist-pump motion.

"From your editor, or is there a half-price sale at Victoria's Secret?" I can't resist teasing, but honestly, I'd be excited about either. I may not let her wear it for long, but I love Cora's newfound addiction to pretty underwear.

"From the magazine!" She's still beaming from ear to ear as she issues a playful swat.

My tongue darts out, an involuntary response I don't try to control anymore. I crave her scent and seeing me capture it turns her on. A double win for me.

She melts into me when I pull her into my arms, her lips parting when I press my mouth to hers. I'm doubly hard by the time I break the kiss, but my never-ending need for her will have to wait.

"*B:Here* extended the monsters column for another year, I assume?" I ask, setting her flat on her fuzzy-pink-slipper-covered feet. "As they should, since it's fantastic and making them tons of affiliate money."

"They did, but it gets even better." She's literally glowing. So fucking beautiful, my Cora. "One of the big New York publishing houses is interested in compiling the articles into a book. A book!" Another shriek fills the room as I scoop her up and spin her around. "Too much, too much!" She burrows in, her face pressed to my chest. "I don't want to get sick again."

I freeze at her words, pulling my head back enough to meet her gaze when she looks up. "What do you mean, sick again? When were you sick? Why didn't you tell me? Have you been to the doctor?"

"So many questions, Daddy."

"Daddy?" I'm not opposed to the term, but it's never been part of our sex life.

She nods, a gentle blush flooding her features as she pulls her bottom lip between her teeth. "To answer all your questions—I've had some nausea for the past couple of weeks, I didn't tell you because I didn't want you to go into 'I can fix this for you' mode, and yes, I had an appointment with the doctor yesterday."

"I will always go into fix-everything mode for you, sweetheart. I wouldn't shut it off if I could. I love you. You're my whole world."

"I love you, too. So much." Her eyelashes flutter wildly as she places her palm on my face.

I know that look. Tears are coming, no matter how hard she tries to hold them back, and my gut coils with fear at the possible reasons. "What did the doctor say?"

"That the day is going to come when I'm not your whole world."

My entire body shakes. "No. We'll get another

doctor. Tests. Treatments. Whatever it takes. I won't lose you, Cora. I can't."

"You're not going to lose me. You're going to gain a little half-me. In about eight months, give or take. There's no way of knowing how long the pregnancy will be, since the baby is part monster."

"Baby," I say, as if it's the first time I've said the word. "You're having a baby."

So many questions, Daddy.

"Technically, yes," she says. "I'll be doing all the heavy lifting on this one, but—"

"No more lifting. Not even shopping bags. I'm doing everything."

"Leroy—"

I shake my head while gently setting her on the couch. "No more motorcycle rides, either."

"But I love the green Monster." Her laugh fills the room, my ears, my heart. "Fine, I'll take a hiatus from riding on your motorcycle. But don't even *think* about trying to deprive me of my *other* green monsters. And before you ask, yes, I already checked with the doctor. As long as it's comfortable for me, it's safe to have sex. All the sex. Any kind I want," she says, waggling her eyebrows.

"I love you, baby." Kneeling between her legs, I lean in and place a kiss below her bellybutton. "And I love you, too, baby." An unfamiliar lump fills my throat as I sit back. "Thank you."

"For what? Having the world's most hospitable uterus?" she asks, giggling. "That was the doctor's best guess for how I got pregnant after they'd told us birth control shouldn't be necessary, since your swimmers probably wouldn't be a good fit with my pond."

"Everything about us is a good fit."

"The best fit." Heat flares in her eyes as she pulls off her sweatshirt to reveal there's nothing underneath. Then she lifts her hips and wiggles her leggings past her hips, down her legs, and off. "No Victoria's Secret today," she says, opening her legs to give me a primo view of her naked pussy. "There's something else you should know about this miracle of pregnancy."

"Tell me." I'm not close enough to lick her, but I taste her arousal on my tongue when it slides out.

"The doctor said not to be surprised if my appetite for more than just food increases."

I'm good with that. Really fucking good. "How's that a miracle?" I ask, unzipping my jeans to free my cocks.

Her gaze travels up and down my body as I strip to the green skin she loves running her hands over. "Because I figure it'll be a miracle if either of us gets any sleep in the next eight months, since I'm already so hungry."

Hard as a fucking rock, I step between her legs. "Hungry? Use your good, dirty words for me, baby."

"Well, I *am* hungry for you," she says, gripping both my shafts and guiding one into her mouth, so deep it makes me hiss a groan. She lets me pop free, licking her lips as she looks up to meet my eyes. "I love sucking you dry. I love the feeling of your cum sliding down my throat."

There's my dirty-talking girl. She's gotten so good at it, she doesn't need my source material anymore.

"But right now, I want something else."

"Anything, baby. I want every fucking thing with you."

"I want both your cocks in me. Both at once," she says, sliding her hand down her body to settle on her clit. "One in my pussy, one in my ass. Like this, so I can see your face when you come inside me."

I drop to my knees and dip my head toward her pussy, but she blocks me with the hand that's rubbing her clit.

"Not that, not now." Her voice is breathy, as if she's halfway there already. She might be, based on the scent and slickness of her pussy. "I'm so horny, I can't wait... I need you inside me, filling me up until I can't breathe."

Fuck. Yes. "I'll be back in ten seconds."

She grabs my arm when I move to grab the lube from the bedroom. "I don't want it slick and easy. I want to really feel you. All of you."

I get positioned between her legs with one cock notched in her pussy. "Get me wet, sweetheart."

Her breath comes out on a gasp as I slide into her heat. "Take me," she says, tipping her hips up after I withdraw.

As if I could ever deny her. I'd never want to. A cock in each hand, I line myself up with her two holes. She's taken both my cocks before, but never without a warmup, and not in this position.

I press against her, groaning at the resistance, at the sight of her arched back and gorgeous tits with their hard, pink peaks. "Breathe, baby. Think about how good it's going to feel when I bury both these cocks inside you."

A heady moan leaves her parted lips as I push deeper, past the tight ring of muscles. *"Leroy..."*

I fucking love it when she says my name while I'm inside her. "That's my good girl," I say, rhythmically rocking in and out, my gaze glued to the sight of my cocks disappearing deeper and deeper into her body. "You're so beautiful, baby." A moan rattles in my chest as I sink the last inches inside her. "You feel so fucking good, I won't last long. Rub that pretty clit and come around my cocks."

"Yes..." she moans, rubbing her clit harder, faster.

Holding her hips, I thrust into her. Shallow strokes that keep me seated deep, and let me feel the tight squeeze of her pussy and ass around me. Fire swirls at the base of my cocks. Jaw clenched, I bite back the urge come. I won't. Not until she does.

"Oh God..." Her breath hitches, her sexy body drawing tight like a bowstring, then writhing and bucking against her fingers and my cocks as she comes.

Gaze locked with hers, I let go, hissing through my release, then folding myself over her while we both fight to catch our breath.

"I love you, Mrs. Shortt."

In the circle of my embrace, she turns to face me as much as our awkward position accommodates.

"You heard me," I say, pressing my mouth to her forehead, the only part I can currently reach. "There's a ring in the office safe, but I don't want to wait the amount of time it'll take to get it. I should've asked you already. I should've asked you the day I bought it. I'm already the luckiest man or monster alive, but I want more. I want everything with you. Please do me the honor of marrying me, sweetheart."

"Yes," she says, the biggest, most beautiful smile lighting her face. "So much yes."

Best day of my life. Again. Because of her. Because of us. And it's only going to get better.

Also by Karla Doyle

Paranormal Romances:

Once Upon A Beast (Hemlock Woods)

The Beast Within (Hemlock Woods)

Mated to the Minotaur (Fate's Falls)

The Grumpy Demon's Sunshine (Fate's Falls)

A Reaper is Forever (Fate's Falls)

The Rhino's Rose (Fate's Falls)

A Dash of Demon (Fate's Falls)

Hell's Belle (Fate's Falls)

Orc-ily Ever After (Fate's Falls)

Falling for the Yeti (Fate's Falls)

A Troll in the Hay (Harmony Glen)

Contemporary Romances:

Dad Bod Wingman (Hope Harbor)

Heart Beats (Hope Harbor)

Last Call Casanova (Hope Harbor)

Fleshing It Out (Hope Harbor)

The Deal With Love (Hope Harbor)

Doggy Style (Hope Harbor)

Resorting to Love (linked to Hope Harbor)

White Lie Christmas (linked to Hope Harbor)

King of Her Dreams (Hope Harbor)

Heart of Texas (linked to Hope Harbor)

Her Pipe Dream (Hope Harbor)

12 Days (Hope Harbor)

Wedded Miss

Puck That

Shifting Gears (Under the Hood)

Driver's Seat (Under the Hood)

Gingerbread Man (Man of the Month: Candy Cane Key)

Just in Queso (Man of the Month: Magnolia Point)

Unexpected Addition

Dating the Doubter

Gift Wrapped

Cup of Sugar (Close to Home #1)

Icing on the Cake (Close to Home #2)

Sweet as Candy (Close to Home #3)

Body of Work (Very Personal Training #1)

Worth the Wait (Very Personal Training #2)

Game Plan

More Than Words

Crossing the Line

A small-town girl with some big-city experience, Karla resides in Southwestern Ontario with her husband and two amazing, young-adult kids. She studied fashion design in college and spent 20+ years working in that industry before succumbing to the writing muse. When she's not writing the sexy stories that swirl around in her head, you can find her spending time with family, hanging out with book-loving friends on Facebook, or cuddled up with a book and her adorable pets.

Karla loves hearing from readers! Connect with her online, or send her an email: karla@karladoyle.com

Join Karla's mailing list to stay up to date on all of her bookish news: www.karladoyle.com/newsletter

Visit Karla's website for more information about her books: www.karladoyle.com

COPYRIGHT

www.ingramcontent.com/pod-product-compliance
Lightning Source LLC
Chambersburg PA
CBHW050358030726
47503CB00006B/1919